Lawless

Derek Taylor

A Black Horse Western

ROBERT HALE · LONDON

© Derek Taylor 2005
First published in Great Britain 2005

ISBN 0 7090 7791 2

Robert Hale Limited
Clerkenwell House
Clerkenwell Green
London EC1R 0HT

Typeset by
Derek Doyle & Associates, Shaw Heath.
Printed and bound in Great Britain by
Antony Rowe Limited, Wiltshire

Lawless

The West Texas town of Pecos is in the grip of lawlessness. Only one man, the young and inexperienced Mitch Miller, has the courage to do anything about it. But first he has to deal with the town's corrupt sheriff, Matt Lock, and his paymaster, a ruthless gambler called Norris.

All seems lost for Miller as he stands alone. Then outlaw Cal Withers and his men ride into town. Withers has no interest in bringing law and order to Pecos but, ironically, there is now just a chance that Miller can clean up the town and stay alive long enough to see it through.

ONE

It was hot. Even for July it was damned hot. The heat wasn't helping Mitch Miller's bad temper any at the events that had been happening with all too much frequency now in Pecos. He'd lived in and around Pecos all his life and barely knew that a world beyond existed save for the coming and going of strangers. Pecos had once been a peaceful haven famed for its cantaloupes, reckoned to be the sweetest in Texas. But, of late, it had become notorious as the roughest frontier town in the West. What was going down in Pecos, though, was the kind of trouble that towns in the West were no longer tolerating. Its citizens may not have liked it but only one of them seemed to have the guts to do anything about it. This was the aforementioned Mitch Miller.

A shot rang out and Miller naturally looked to see where it came from. A few yards down Main Street was the Broken Spoke saloon. Miller looked just in time to see a man come flying out of it. It was obvious from the way his arms were thrown out that he'd been shot in the chest. As the shot man hit the ground Miller stood up. The man's chest was spilling blood from three bullet holes. Miller watched as the man breathed his last. He wanted to do something about it. Sheriff Lock was out of town, which, he thought, was just as well, since he knew if he were there he'd do nothing about it. He was a time-server who for his own corrupt reasons did nothing while the town went to rack and ruin. Miller had had enough of it. Should he do something about it? Had the time come? Was it now?

As his mind grappled with the dilemma he saw in another man came flying out of the Broken Spoke. This one was firing back into the saloon. As the man ran for cover, a cowpoke that Miller recognized came running out after him. Miller watched people, ordinary citizens of Pecos, run for cover, as a gun battle ensued. It wasn't right, he thought, that they should have to put up with this. His horse was tied up to a hitching rail nearby. Stepping up to it, he pulled a Winchester .44-44 rifle from its saddle holster. Putting a bullet into the breech, he stepped on to Main Street.

The gun battle that had raged between the two men who had come out of the saloon suddenly seemed to go quiet. Miller wondered if it was because they had seen him or if it was because they had run out of ammunition. Miller didn't care which. He'd had enough. He was no lawman and he had no right to stop these two men doing whatever they wanted in Pecos, but he was damned if he was going to sit by and watch the ordinary decent folk of Pecos take it any more. As he looked around him he could see that the town's plank-walks were deserted. He could still hear the sounds of rowdiness coming from the Broken Spoke saloon but the rest of the town was suddenly deathly quiet.

'Norris,' he called out to the man he had recognized, 'throw down your gun and step out with your hands up.'

Norris, who had taken cover behind a water-butt on the corner of a building next to the Broken Spoke, had no intention of obeying Miller. He had just reloaded his Colt .44 and still had more than a dozen bullets stashed in his gun belt: more than enough to deal with Miller.

'Stay out of what don't concern you,' he called back to Miller.

Miller knew Norris to be a lowlife cowboy who had been thrown off every ranch in the county for being less than useless and a bad influence on the other men. He lived now by fleecing drunken innocents at poker in the Broken Spoke and sharing his winnings with the owner. Sometimes his victims weren't as innocent or as drunk as they seemed and the kind of thing that was happening now followed. If someone got killed, and they often did, Norris was always able to claim self-defence and Sheriff Lock, a close friend of the Broken Spoke's owner, Zeb Turner, always accepted it.

'I just don't like ya,' was Miller's reply, 'and the things you and your kind are doing to my town.'

'Sorree!' Norris sang out in mocking tones.

By now word had begun to spread round the Broken Spoke that something was happening outside on Main Street. Slowly people began to spill out on to the plank-walk.

'You will be,' Miller replied, 'if you don't throw down your gun and step out with your hands up.'

'Since when did you become the law in these parts?'

'Since I decided that I wasn't gonna wait any longer for Lock to do the job the town pays him for.'

The fact that he and Miller now had an audience made Norris all the more determined to face Miller down. If he lost face here, he'd lose all credibility in the Broken Spoke and his scamming days there would be over. He had friends in the Broken Spoke; one of them, surely, he hoped, would come to his aid. In the meantime he had to brave it out. Beads of sweat began to form on his forehead. Miller was known to him but he had never seen him in action and didn't know how fast he was with a gun.

'Is that right now?' he asked.

Miller didn't reply. Instead he simply lifted his rifle shoulder-high, pointed it at Norris and cocked it. Norris suddenly realized he was in a dangerously disadvantaged position.

'All right,' he declared. 'I'll tell you what I'll do. I'll let this cheating cowpoke go.'

He was obviously referring to the man he'd been having the gunfight with.

'Go on,' he shouted to the man, not taking his eyes off Miller. 'Clear off. Now. Before I change my mind.'

Taking advantage of what to him was a welcome reprieve, the man broke cover and looking nervously over his shoulder ran off down Main Street.

'There,' remarked Norris. 'That satisfy you?'

'There's still him,' Miller replied, indicating the dead body lying in the dirt not far from him. 'I can't rest with him on my conscience.'

This exasperated Norris. Miller was intent on making trouble, he reckoned, and it began to get to him. Just then one of his sidekicks pushed his way through the crowd that had collected on the plank-walk outside the Broken Spoke. He was waving a gun in the air.

'Go for it, Ben,' Norris shouted to him, raising his gun to fire at what he hoped would be a momentarily distracted Miller.

Miller, though, was not so easily put off his stride. He'd been wanting an opportunity like this to arise for some time. Now that it had arisen he wasn't going to waste it. Closing his finger on the trigger of his rifle he let off a shot that knocked Norris's gun out of his hand. Then, turning to the other man, who was by now on the steps of the plank-walk, he let go another shot. It too slammed into the man's shooting hand, sending his gun flying as it had done Norris's. As the man grabbed his bloodied wrist, the crowd, taking fright, all began to push their way back into the saloon.

Miller turned to look back at Norris. But he was not there. Miller guessed he must have run up an alley between the Broken Spoke and the building served by the water butt he'd hidden behind. Looking back to see what the other man was doing, he saw that he, too, had fled. Miller guessed he'd done enough for the time being and decided to go find the undertaker to take away the dead body. For the rest, he knew that Sheriff Lock and his paymasters would have something to say about what had just happened and it was more than likely not going to be to his or the town's liking. Well, they could take whatever action they wanted but this time they'd learn that if it wasn't the right action there'd be consequences.

TWO

The owner of the Broken Spoke saloon, Zeb Turner, was indignant. He wanted to know who the hell Miller thought he was.

'Miller's Miller and he ain't a kid anymore,' Jim Wood, the owner of the general store in Pecos, remarked. He had stepped into the Broken Spoke shortly after the day's happenings.

'What do you mean by that?'

'Just that he's one of those people who don't like things not being as they ought.'

'Matt's the sheriff,' Turner replied emphatically, thinking of the money he paid Lock every week to turn a blind eye to the goings on in the saloon.

'People getting pretty fed up with his inability to control the town. Maybe it's time we had a change. As I said, things is getting out of hand.'

Jim Wood knew he was speaking to the man who stood to gain the most from things remaining as they were in Pecos and he hoped his words put him on notice that things weren't going to stay as they were just because he wanted them to. He didn't dislike Turner, just hated the way he and others had Sheriff Lock in their pockets.

'We go letting people take the law into their own hands and we'll have complete anarchy on our hands,' Turner said in the kind of slippery tones that did not fool Jim Wood.

'Maybe we ought to call a meeting of the town council and put it to the vote. It hired Lock, it can just as easily sack him.'

Turner suddenly felt panicky and it showed in his face.

'I don't think there's any need for that,' he declared. 'Lock'll be back in town tomorrow. We can have a word with him and I'm sure he'll put things right.'

Jim Wood merely grunted in reply. He knew

what having a word with Lock would amount to and knew it wouldn't change things one little bit.

'Whatever,' Turner, seeing he wasn't convincing Wood, remarked, re-stating things as he saw them, 'the town can't tolerate people taking the law into their own hands and Miller's gonna have to be told that.'

Again Jim Wood just grunted in reply. He was standing at the bar and Zeb Turner had poured him a glass of whiskey, which, as they talked, he'd been turning around with the fingers of his right hand. He stopped now, looked at the shot-glass and downed the drink in one go. Then he turned to leave.

'Maybe I'll have a word with Miller myself,' he said. 'Sound him out. See if he'd consider taking on the job of sheriff. If there were to be a vacancy, that is.'

He was walking out of the saloon before Turner had a chance to reply. It left Turner feeling more uneasy than ever. He was paying off his own gambling debts and his profits were piling up nicely. Another year or two and he'd have enough to buy the little ranch in East Texas he'd always dreamed of retiring to. He didn't want anyone doing anything that might alter that.

Meantime Miller was in the house of the woman he loved, Hannah Voegel. She was a young widow who lived in a small house at the end of Main Street. Her husband had been a doctor but, ironically, soon after taking up residence in Pecos he had himself taken sick and died. He left her penniless but for the house they'd built and she took in sewing. There was precious little of it but she made enough to get by on.

She and Miller were just finishing dinner.

'More coffee?' she asked him, lifting the coffee-pot from the stove.

She hardly needed to ask him, knowing that he normally at any time could drink the coffee-pot dry.

'Thank you, honey,' Miller replied, sitting back contentedly in his chair and using his tongue to remove food noisily from between his teeth.

'I wish you wouldn't do that, Mitch,' Hannah, refilling his coffee-cup, chided him. 'It's so vulgar.'

He reached out to wind an arm around her waist as she went to put the coffee-pot back on the stove.

'I'm sorry, Hannah, darling,' he replied. 'I always forget how fine your Eastern manners are.'

'It's got nothing to do with Eastern manners. It's just manners.'

Miller let her go and smiled to himself. He blessed his good fortune in finding so lovely and feminine a woman as Hannah to make his own. Having her was one of the reasons he wanted to clean up Pecos. As it stood, it wasn't fit for a woman as sweet and precious as his gal. Some months back a stray bullet had killed a woman walking along Main Street. Now a townswoman hardly dare step out of her house, for fear of suffering the same fate.

Hannah knew what had happened that afternoon and she was worried.

'When's Sheriff Lock due back in town?' she asked Miller.

He knew why she was asking, knew what her concerns were.

'Tomorrow, should be. He's gone to Odessa. To bank his ill-gotten gains, I wouldn't be surprised. He don't like to bank in Pecos, just in case people find out how much he's making. But honey, what you worrying about when he gets back?'

'Because he might try to arrest you for shooting those two men,' Hannah replied in anxious tones.

'You don't want to go worrying your little head about that,' Miller said, turning in his chair to face her and reaching out his arms to pull her towards him. 'I was making a citizen's arrest and only shot in self-defence. Enough people witnessed it. I'll be all right.'

He didn't really believe it was that simple but he didn't care much either. He was tougher than that.

'But what if Sheriff Lock doesn't see it like that?' Hannah asked him.

'Well,' he sighed, 'I'll deal with that when it happens.'

'And if the men you shot come looking for you?'

'I'll deal with that, too, when it happens,' was his reply, pulling Hannah ever closer to him.

She was tense and he wanted to reassure

her. Looking her in the face, he said:

'Look, Hannah. This town ain't safe for a lady like you to walk in. You think I'm gonna put up with that? But don't worry, them cowpokes is mostly drunk. They couldn't shoot straight if they tried. And if they come looking for me, I'll be ready for them.'

Miller was taller than Hannah and she nestled her head in his shoulder.

'I've already lost one good man, Mitch,' she said. 'I don't want to lose another.'

'You won't, honey, I promise you that,' was his reply.

As Miller spoke, half a mile away Norris stepped into the Broken Spoke saloon. His shooting hand was bandaged, but he could shoot just as well with his left, as he had a mind to show anyone who got in his way that evening. He hoped it was going to be Miller.

THREE

Norris didn't find the trouble he was looking for in the Broken Spoke saloon that night and the next day Sheriff Matt Lock returned to town. Zeb Turner told him what had gone down.

'You saying Miller shot Norris and Norris ain't done nothin' about it yet?' Lock asked him incredulously.

'So far nothin' ain't happened, but the way Norris is talking it ain't gonna be long before something does.'

'Ach, let them get on with it,' Sheriff Lock, true to character, remarked suddenly. 'We're best leaving them all to shoot it out amongst themselves.'

'I don't think so. Not this time,' someone

21

was heard to say. It was Jim Wood. He'd seen Lock come riding up to the saloon and go in. 'Town's getting sick of it, Matt. We don't want no more murders and we don't want no more trouble.'

Sheriff Lock, time-serving coward that he was, was unnerved by what he heard.

'Your store doing good business?' he asked Wood.

It was but Wood didn't see that this was the point.

'Well, is it?' Lock asked.

'I can't complain,' Wood replied.

'Well, then don't,' Lock said, indicating to Turner that he wanted a drink.

'I'd do more if folk from round about thought they could come into town without risking their necks,' Wood continued. 'People are saying if you can't make Pecos safe for decent folk, then maybe Miller can, Matt. He's already shown he's got the nerve for it.'

'You saying I ain't,' Lock said, turning on him and knocking back in one hit the whiskey Turner had poured for him.

'A man was shot dead, Matt,' Wood informed him in case he hadn't already been told.

'For cheating at cards,' Turner reminded him.

'And, from what I understand, Miller took the law into his own hands,' Lock said. 'Guess that makes everyone square. If I'm gonna arrest Norris, I gotta arrest Miller, too. And Zeb here says Norris shot in self-defence; what's gonna be Miller's excuse?'

Zeb Turner looked at Sheriff Lock as if to say 'did I say that?' It seemed a good excuse for doing nothing but he wasn't sure he'd thought it up.

'I don't know if that's how the town will see it, let alone Miller, but you're the sheriff, Matt, for the time being anyway,' Wood said.

'What d'you mean "for the time-being",' Lock asked, rounding on him.

'What I said, Matt. You men have got greedy. Town don't like it and they ain't gonna let you get away with it any more. Not now it's hurting them so much.'

Turner could sense that things were getting heated and thought he ought to try and calm them down a bit.

'Let's all just have a drink,' he suggested.

Wood would have liked to wet his whistle

but he declined the offer.

'Too early in the day for me,' he pretended. 'Got work to do.'

'Go and do it, then, Jim,' Lock said to him, 'and leave the law-keeping to me. That's what the town pays me for, ain't it?'

Jim Wood knew the answer he'd liked to give in reply but he reckoned he'd be wasting his breath. Instead he simply turned and walked out of the saloon. Lock and Turner merely looked at one another. They said nothing for a moment and then Turner spoke.

'Guess we got some fast thinking to do, Matt. Else it's all gonna start to unravel for us.'

Lock continued to say nothing. He wasn't brave enough to be thinking in the way Turner would have liked him to be.

Later in the day Norris was back in the Broken Spoke boasting that he was going to make Miller pay for what he'd done. The bandage on his right hand was looking grubby and his fingers were swollen. His sidekick Ben Kirk was at his side, egging him on. They both wanted to know where Miller was.

'Why doesn't the lily-livered ladies' man show his face?' Norris asked.

'Guess he will when he's a mind to,' someone was heard to say.

'That's if he ain't too afraid to,' Kirk, remarked.

'Table's waiting.' Turner interrupted them, indicating to Norris that a group of cowboys was waiting for him to start dealing.

Norris looked at his wounded hand. Dealing wasn't going to be easy but he guessed it was what he should do.

'Yeah,' was all he said in reply, adding for Ben Kirk's benefit, 'Guess that's the other thing we're here to do.'

It had been another hot day and the evening had not yet brought much respite. No one in the place was fresh. Everyone in the Broken Spoke reeked of stale sweat but no one noticed; they didn't usually smell of anything else. The good-time girls could have wished for something better, but everyone was making money, so why should any of them care?

Not even the madame. She made more than most. She hated Norris but knew that it was through him most of the money cheated from unsuspecting drunken cowboys came. She sidled up to him now.

'That hand of yours looks nasty, Norry. I hope you're taking care of it,' she remarked, standing beside him and running a hand over his shoulders to show she cared.

'It's nothing, Kate,' Norris declared, putting a brave face on it, though blushing some.

He was making more than a competent job of dealing the cards with his left hand.

'Well, don't you go letting it get infected,' Kate insisted in affectionate tones.

'My hand ain't no better,' Ben Kirk remarked soppily, hoping Kate would fuss over him some.

'Well, now,' Kate said, changing her tone from indulgent softness to matronly concern, 'you just look after it, too.'

Then, after running a hand through Norris's hair, she left them to their game of cards, smiling seductively at the gathered players as she left. This had the intended effect of making them all less guarded and more susceptible to being cheated. All of them except one, that was. He'd never had any interest in the ladies and only lived to gamble and drink. He'd been steadily piling up his winnings but now suddenly there were not enough spots on his cards and he reckoned he could see why.

'I saw that!' he suddenly snarled at Norris.

'What'd you see?' Norris snapped back at him, pausing to stop dealing and looking the man squarely between the eyes.

'I saw you pull a card from under the pack!'

Norris's tactic was never to wait for the argument to develop and never to suffer the indignity of defending himself. If someone accused him of cheating the sooner they died for their audacity the better. It taught others to think twice before taking a stand against him.

'Oh yeah?' he suddenly snarled, jumping up from his chair and causing the table nearly to turn over as he did so. As the players instinctively put their hands over their money to safeguard it, he reached for his gun with his good hand and continued: 'You gonna carry on in that vain and die or are you gonna get out of here?'

The player pondered the matter as Norris stood looming over him. He was wearing a gun. There was a rule that no one was supposed to wear their weapons in town but it had not been obeyed for months and particularly not since Lock had been made sheriff.

The player might have been wearing a gun but it was more for decorative purposes than anything. He knew he wasn't any good with it and wasn't prepared to risk drawing against someone with Norris's reputation for notching up killings. He'd been in the saloon the night before and had seen what could happen. He decided to take what was left of his winnings and go. Not as steady on his legs as a serious gambler should be, he got to his feet, took off his hat, pulled his money into it and backed off from the table.

Norris let out a roar of mocking laughter and sat back down again, putting his gun on the table in front of him.

'Now,' he asked, 'anyone else got any complaints they wanna make?'

None of the other players had. Expecting it to be the case, he declared: 'Well, let's play on, then.'

The player, hating being humiliated the way he had been, pushed his way to the bar and demanded a drink from Zeb Turner.

'I don't know about giving you a drink,' Turner informed him, 'I ought to bar you for even suggesting I run a bent establishment.'

'Well, don't that just about beat it all!' the gambler exclaimed.

He turned to look for some sort of moral support from the people around him but none was forthcoming. They were too busy revelling to pay any attention to him.

'Get out and go buy your drink elsewhere,' Turner ordered him.

This was too much for the gambler. He slammed his hat on to the bar top, pulled his gun from its holster and ordered Turner to serve him.

'Give me a bottle of whiskey or I'll kill ya,' he ordered.

Turner kept a loaded shotgun under the counter but he wasn't sure he'd be able to get to it in time. Equally he knew he couldn't risk losing face in front of his customers. A tense moment followed as people around the gambler began to stand back.

'I said pour me a drink,' the gambler demanded again.

But his patience had run out and when it became obvious to him that Turner was not going to comply he began to shoot up the bar behind him. Turner ducked down and made a grab for his shotgun. He came up shooting and sent the gambler to kingdom come with a shot that blew his face and most of his head off.

Flesh, brains and blood splattered the people nearest him. Horrified the whole bar went quiet. Except for Norris, who had stood up the moment he heard gunfire. He had been pushing his way through the crowd when Turner had shot the gambler and a large part of the back of the man's head had splattered the front of his jacket.

'God!' he snarled looking down at himself in false disgust. 'Ain't there nowhere civilized in this town a man can play a game of poker without having to put up with this kind of thing?'

None of the people around him replied. They all knew him and thought the remark a bit rich coming from him, but none of them would have dared say so. Precious few of them even cared to. The only one who did was the madame, Kate.

'Come on, Norrie,' she said walking up to him, 'let's get you cleaned up.'

'Cleaned up?' Norris snarled, 'what the hell do I want to get cleaned up for? I like being covered in dead men's brains.'

'Aw, Norrie . . .' Kate tried again to soothe him.

'I said shut up, woman,' Norris said, snarling some more. 'Only thing wrong with these brains is they're the wrong man's.'

Those who knew him and who knew what had happened the day before guessed what he was referring to. Kate had thought of a reply, but before she could get it out, Norris began to push past her, saying:

'In fact I am gonna go find that sonofabitch now and do to him what I ought to have done yesterday.'

Kate didn't even try to stop him. She knew there'd be no point. Norris was a pig. Let him grunt all he wanted, she thought to herself as she watched him go careering through the saloon's batwings. Hot on his heels was Ben Kirk.

FOUR

Norris walked straight into the path of Sheriff Lock. Sheriff Lock had been passing on the other side of Main Street when the shooting had started in the saloon. True to his nature he'd waited for it to stop before going over to see what it was all about. He could have guessed and, seeing Norris now, he knew that his guess would have been right.

'You arrested that sonofabitch Miller yet?' Norris barked at him.

Sheriff Lock began to mutter something in reply but Norris shut him up.

'Didn't think so,' he said. 'Guess I am gonna have to do it for you,' he added.

Sheriff Lock was looking with distaste at

what he saw was splattered all over Norris's front.

'Is that what I think it is, Norris?' he asked.

Norris, who had begun to calm down, looked down at himself.

'Sure is.' Ben Kirk smirked, feeding off what he considered was Norris's heroically hard ways. 'There's a body back there that wants half a head to be made whole again.'

Lock wasn't impressed, though. He was a coward and feared lest Norris took out some of his anger on him.

'I want Miller,' Norris said to him. 'No one does this to me and gets away with it,' he added lifting up his right hand to show Lock what he was talking about.

'Nor me,' chimed in Kirk, holding up his own injured hand.

'You'll get him,' Lock said trying to reassure Norris, while ignoring Kirk. 'It's just that I ain't seen him yet. But I heard what he done and he ain't gonna get away with it. I'm the law round here and no one else, and I aim to let Miller know it.'

Norris gave Lock a contemptuous look. He'd calmed down enough now to want to take up

Kate's offer of getting cleaned up.

'Best you do and soon, Matt,' he said in waspish tones, before turning to walk back into the saloon.

Lock was going to follow him but thought better of it. Instead he turned to walk back to his office. A few minutes later he could have wished he hadn't. He'd come face to face with Miller who happened to be walking down Main Street with Jim Wood.

'Jim,' Lock said to Jim Wood by way of a greeting. Turning to Miller, he said: 'Seems like I missed something important going on yesterday. I hear you shot two men.'

'If you was doing your job, Sheriff, I wouldn't have had to,' Miller replied.

'Yeah, but you did shoot them and I gotta arrest you for it.'

'And what about arresting the man who started the trouble and who no doubt's causing the trouble in there now?' Wood said, indicating with a tilt of his head the Broken Spoke saloon.

'From what I hear Norris shot the man in self-defence,' Lock said. 'There was a gun battle.'

'Why is it,' Wood asked, 'Norris is always in the right and everyone else is in the wrong?'

'Guess people don't like losing at cards,' Lock replied.

'If they weren't wearing guns, they couldn't go starting gunfights and Pecos would be a safer place for its citizens,' Miller remarked.

'Well you ain't exactly helping things in that direction, now, are you, Miller. If you want to disarm the town, how about starting with giving me your weapon,' Lock replied, holding a hand out to receive it.

'I'll give up my gun when the town's got a lawman who can do his job.'

'Well, in that case, I suppose I'm going to have to arrest you on two charges,' Sheriff Lock declared.

'Matt, that ain't the answer. Miller ain't the trouble in this town and you know it.'

'Shut up, Jim,' Lock suddenly snapped at him, drawing his gun. 'Stick to storekeeping. It's what you know best.'

Turning on Miller he demanded of him he gave up his gun. Miller hesitated. Lock had the advantage. Miller knew that if he tried to draw on him he wouldn't stand a chance. But at the same time he didn't see why he should give up his weapon when the likes of Norris were allowed to keep theirs.

'I ain't gonna give it to you, Lock, and leave myself defenceless in a town you ain't got the mind to make safe for ordinary citizens,' he said.

Before Lock could make a reply the batwings of the Broken Spoke saloon flew open and two men threw the corpse of the gambler Zeb Turner had shot out into the middle of Main Street. It caught both Miller and Lock's attention. It was an opportunity for Wood to get between them and he took it.

'Don't you think you'd do better going and see seeing what that's all about?' he said to Lock, stepping forward to stand in front of him.

Lock looked from Miller to the gambler's corpse and back again. He already knew what had happened in the Broken Spoke but didn't let on. He just hoped Norris didn't come out of the saloon. He didn't want to get involved in what would almost certainly degenerate into a shootout between Norris and Miller.

'All right,' he said to Miller, 'but you ain't

getting away with it. I'll come looking for you later.'

Miller said nothing in reply and Sheriff Lock, with gun still in hand, turned and walked over to where the gambler's corpse had landed.

'Reckon the time has come to call a town council meeting. You talk as if you might have something to say to them,' Wood remarked to Miller, breathing a sigh of relief, glad that the potentially deadly situation that was developing between him and Norris had been averted. For the time being, at least.

'Yeah, well something's gotta be done, Jim, before the good citizens of this town start taking more than just the law into their own hands. If Lock can't do the job the town's paying him for, then maybe I can.'

Giving Miller a long, hard look, Wood knew what he was implying.

'If you're sure,' Wood said.

'I'm sure as I'll ever be about anything,' Miller replied, thinking of his sweetheart Hannah Voegel.

As Miller and Wood turned to walk away, Lock was standing looking in horror at what used to be the gambler's head. He'd take comfort later in ascertaining that it was Turner and not Norris who had shot the man and that it was again done in self-defence.

FIVE

Other citizens of the town, taking Miller's lead, began to come forward demanding the removal of Sheriff Lock from his post. One of them was Dwight Cash, the town's blacksmith. He and Jim Wood were egging Miller on to put himself forward as town sheriff to replace the discredited Lock.

'Well, Mitch, what d'you think?' Wood asked him.

'It ain't gonna be as easy as you seem to think, and I gotta know the whole town's behind me,' was Miller's reply.

'It will be. Lock's had his chance. I said right from the start he'd be no good,' Cash put in. He was as dark, big and brawny as you'd expect a blacksmith to be. 'I feel like going into the Broken Spoke and sorting the place out myself.'

Both Miller and Wood knew he could if he wanted.

'Everyone knows what you did the other day, Mitch, and people are mighty proud of you,' Jim Wood remarked.

'They said before that I was too young.'

'Yeah, but people know now it ain't how old you are, it's what you're made of.'

Miller was silent for a moment. Then he said: 'You know Lock says he's gonna arrest me.'

Cash and Wood looked at one another and smiled.

'You really think he means to?' Cash asked him.

'He ain't got the balls to,' Wood added.

'Well, while he remains sheriff he still could.'

'Well, let's see if he does. If he don't before the council meeting, he won't ever get the chance to. Now, you gonna take the job or not?'

Miller was pensively silent for a moment. Then, with resolution in his voice, he replied:

'All right. I will. But I'm gonna need some deputies.'

'You'll get all the help you want,' Wood reassured him.

'From where and whom?' Miller asked.

'Me, for one,' Dwight Cash informed him. 'I'm as fed up with life in this town being ruined by what goes on in the Broken Spoke as everyone else and I'm prepared to help anyone who's willing to try and stop Norris and his pals.'

'You know it'll be dangerous work, helping me to try and clean up this town, don't ya,' Miller said to him.

'I do,' Cash replied, 'but no more dangerous, at least for my wife and children, than letting things continue as they are.'

They were in Jim Wood's store and it was the day after Zeb Turner had splattered Norris's shirt with the brains of the non-compliant gambler. They talked some more, then Cash said he had to get back to work. Miller said he ought to be getting on too and both men took their leave of Jim Wood. Jim Wood said he'd be calling a meeting of the town council and hoped it'd be in a day or two at the most. Miller and Cash acknowledged what he said with looks rather than words, then both stepped out on to the plank-walk outside Wood's store. They said they'd see one another later and then walked off in opposite directions along Main Street.

Miller's path took him by the Broken Spoke. He came level with it just in time to come up against Sheriff Lock, who was coming through the saloon's batwing doors.

Both men came to a halt and looked one another in the eye. Miller remembered that Lock had said he was going to arrest him; Lock thought that he must but knew Miller would resist it.

'I gotta arrest you, Miller,' Lock suddenly declared, throwing his voice over his shoulder hoping that Norris, who was standing by the bar in the saloon, would hear him. Norris did hear it and decided he wanted to join in.

'Yeah,' Miller replied to Lock, who by now was standing on the plank-walk outside the Broken Spoke saloon. 'Well, come on then and try.'

Lock didn't look about to take any kind of decisive action. He wasn't minded to try anything alone and was relieved to hear someone, who, he hoped, was Norris, come through the batwing doors behind him. Seeing that it *was* Norris, Lock suddenly took heart and told Miller to take his gun out of his holster and throw it to the ground in front of him.

Miller had no intention of obeying him. Particularly after the appearance of Norris.

'You heard the sheriff,' Norris suddenly declared, not waiting to see what Miller's intentions were. 'Drop your gun or else.'

Miller knew he had to keep his nerve or he was lost.

'Ain't he the one you oughta be arresting?' Miller asked Lock, obviously meaning Norris.

'Norris ain't broken the law, you have,' Lock replied.

He didn't sound authoritative and looked unconvincing in trying to be.

Miller said nothing in reply but simply threw Lock and Norris a look of contempt.

'Looks like you're gonna have to take his gun,' Norris informed Lock.

'I ain't gonna ask you a third time. Now throw down your gun,' Lock ordered Miller.

'What you arresting me for, Lock?' Miller asked him.

'This,' Norris, speaking for Lock, replied between gritted teeth, holding his injured hand up in the air. 'This,' he repeated.

Jim Wood had noticed that Miller had been waylaid outside the Broken Spoke and decided he might be needed there.

'Now, you gonna do as the sheriff here tells you or is someone gonna have to make you?' Norris snarled at Miller.

Wood, who had left his shop to walk over to where Miller was standing, soon guessed what was happening.

'Miller ain't gonna do nothing,' he informed Norris. 'At least nothing you've gotta a mind to poke your nose in. Now back off, Norris, and let him go about his business.'

'And who's gonna make me? You?' Norris replied sneeringly.

'No, I will,' a voice called out from the end of the plank-walk.

It was that of Dwight Cash, who had appeared from an alley between the Broken Spoke saloon and the building next to it. He was holding a shotgun, the double barrels of which he had pointed in Lock's direction. Slowly he cocked the triggers.

Norris and Lock turned to look in the direction from which Cash's words came.

'Well, my, ain't we got ourselves a gathering here,' Norris remarked on seeing Cash.

Lock simply looked defeated. He didn't know what to do next. Miller helped him out of his dilemma.

'Thanks, Jim, Dwight,' he said, touching his hat graciously. 'I'm mighty obliged.'

He turned and began to walk away, saying mockingly to Lock: 'Another time perhaps, eh, Sheriff?'

Miller had turned his back on them but Norris had decided he wasn't going to let him get away that easily. With lightning speed, even though using his left hand, he went for his gun. Cash saw it, and, having his shotgun already cocked, was even quicker. Pellets from one of its barrels slammed into a wooden post a few inches from Norris's head. Norris had got a shot off but it went wide and hit who knew what or where.

On hearing first Norris's and then Cash's gun discharge, Miller turned sharply on his heels, drawing his own gun as he did so. He knew a gunshot sound when he heard one and quickly realized Cash had fired at Norris who had obviously fired at him. He eyeballed Norris, who, he reckoned, was looking decidedly unnerved, and thought he could leave Cash to finish what he'd started, or prevented, if you looked at it that way. He slowly replaced his gun in its holster and, then, tipping his hat in thanks to Cash, and throwing Lock one last look of contempt, he slowly turned and continued walking away.

'You can walk away now,' Norris called after him, 'but you won't always be able to. Just remember that.'

Miller ignored him.

'And you,' Norris continued, turning on Cash, 'you're dead. Deader than Miller.'

Cash said nothing in reply but simply kept a stubbornly defiant stare fixed on Norris. Norris eyeballed him back but then suddenly turned and stomped back into the Broken Spoke saloon, violently pushing open the batwing doors. When Norris had gone Cash turned a withering look on Lock. Lock barely looked back. Instead he turned and slinked off along the plank-walk in the direction of his office.

'You weren't pretending, were you, Dwight,' Jim Wood suddenly spoke up, 'when you said you'd be there?'

'No, I wasn't,' was all Cash said in reply, lowering his shotgun and fingering the untriggered hammer gently back into place. 'And Norris best believe it,' he added, turning to walk away.

SIX

Norris went back into the Broken Spoke saloon fulminating against Miller and insisting again that he was 'dead, dead, dead!' He almost bumped into Ben Kirk, who was coming to see what had been going on outside. Kirk asked Norris what had happened but Norris merely kept on fulminating against Miller, then Cash and next Lock, whom he labelled yellow as mustard but without the bite.

'Yeah,' Kirk agreed with him, 'you ain't wrong.'

Ignoring Kirk, Norris pushed his way past him to the bar. Turner saw him coming and set up for him a bottle of redeye and a shot glass. He poured for Norris the first drink from the bottle.

'There ain't no point in wasting any more time waiting for Lock to arrest the sonofabitch,' Norris declared to Turner, taking the shot-glass in his good hand and knocking back its contents in one go. 'I'm gonna have to make him pay for this myself,' he added, holding his injured hand up for Turner to see.

'Perhaps you better had,' Turner replied, 'before things get any more out of hand. Lock ain't gonna be sheriff for much longer, that's obvious, unless we fix it so that there's no one else to take his place.'

Norris indicated his agreement and Turner refilled his shot-glass.

Meanwhile Miller had made his way to Hannah Voegel's house. Despite having faced down Norris, he was feeling uneasy, wondering what was going to happen next and how he was going to deal with it. He knew he wouldn't always be able to count on Jim Wood or Dwight Cash showing up when he needed them most.

Hannah Voegel had prepared a meal for him. He decided he wouldn't tell her about what had just happened. Gunfire was nothing

out of the ordinary in town and she didn't
need to know that he been involved in it.
She'd only start to think her worst fears were
beginning to be realized. Instead he simply
sat down at the table she'd prepared for him,
commenting on how good the meal smelled.
She gave him a linen napkin. As he spread it
across his lap in readiness to eat, six men on
horseback rode into town.

SEVEN

The six riders were led by a man called Cal Withers. He decided that before they did what they'd come to Pecos to do they'd rest up for a day. There was one hotel in town. It was called Millie's Hotel. Withers and his men dismounted at the hitching rail adjacent to it and went straight in. Millie's Hotel was opposite Jim Wood's store and he saw the six men go in.

It wasn't unusual to see strangers ride into town but there was something about these six riders that made Jim Wood think. They had an air of disciplined purposefulness about them, rather than the usual devil-may-care-I'm-out-for-a-good-time abandonment that was normal.

Many thoughts raced through his head

about what their purpose might be. Not the least of them was one that made him wonder if they had been sent for. Someone ought to find out. That someone, he thought, should be Mitch Miller, who he couldn't help but think of now as the town's sheriff-in-waiting. He decided he had to go and find him.

He found him in Hannah Voegel's. It was just gone two in the afternoon and he'd had lunch there. After exchanging polite greetings with Hannah, he told Miller he needed to talk to him.

'Sure thing,' Miller replied, reaching for his gun belt and hat.

Miller said goodbye to Hannah and the two men left.

'What is it?' Miller asked Wood, as they began to walk towards the main part of town.

'Maybe something, maybe nothing,' Wood replied, 'I don't know. But six men just rode into town.'

'What's so unusual about that?' Miller asked, perplexed.

'They're different, Mitch. They had an air about them that was out of the ordinary.'

'Is that right?' Miller asked.

'Yeah,' Wood replied. 'And they went straight to Millie's.'

'You mean they didn't make a beeline for the Broken Spoke?'

'Yeah,' Wood replied.

Miller thought for a moment.

'What do you think they're in town for?' he asked Wood.

'That's what I thought you could find out. I mean, maybe they was sent for.'

'By who?' Miller asked, suddenly even more perplexed by the matter.

'Well, that's what I thought,' was Wood's reply.

'Things ain't got that far yet,' Miller remarked, obviously referring to the impending removal of Lock from his post. 'Besides, who would take it upon themselves to do such a thing?'

'Exactly, Mitch. But I gotta a feeling about it. Maybe you oughta wander into Millie's and just see if it is something or nothing.'

Miller said that he would. By the time he and Wood had finished talking they'd reached Wood's store. Both men stood and looked across at Millie's Hotel.

'Could be Lock or Turner sent for them. Or even Norris for that matter,' Wood remarked.

'Could be,' was all Miller said in reply. He turned and looked at Wood. 'Guess we'll soon find out,' he added, turning and stepping off the plank-walk to cross Main Street and enter Millie's Hotel. Wood watched him go and then turned and walked into his store.

Millie, who would not normally be seen at that hour of the day, was standing in the lobby when Miller walked in.

'Mitch!' she greeted him, 'how nice to see you!'

Millie was nothing if she were not ebullient. Her establishment was not like that of the Broken Spoke saloon. It was more show business and less a rampant watering hole. Consequently it attracted a better class of client, though business had dropped off somewhat of late. This was due, Millie had no doubt, to the lawlessness that was infecting Pecos. Nice people weren't coming in the numbers they used to any more; they were going to Odessa.

Still, Millie managed to keep up appearances and as she and Miller greeted one another her showgirls were on stage rehearsing for the evening's music hall performance.

Miller exchanged a few further pleasantries with Millie, then got to the point. Millie said that she didn't know who the six riders were, just that they had walked into her hotel and booked in for a night.

'They're a mighty distinguished looking bunch, particularly their leader,' she commented. 'I don't think we're gonna have any trouble from them.'

'You say they're upstairs in their rooms now? Miller asked.

'Yeah, taking a bath, each and every one of them,' was Millie's reply.

Miller mused for a moment, then Millie asked him: 'Why all the interest, Mitch?'

'Well, you know what's going on in town with Lock. We're used to cowpokes and lowlife riding into town and joining in the goings-on at the Spoke, but these men? That's something different. I just wondered if there was something in it.'

'I was mighty surprised to see them come trooping in myself,' Millie replied, 'but I could see they was different and there was no obvious bad in them, otherwise I would have turned them away.'

Miller acknowledged the meaning of what Millie said and then took his leave. He said he'd be back later when he might be able to get a look at the men for himself.

'Well, you do that,' Millie sang out to him. 'And come and see the show. You haven't been in here for a long time, Mitch, and we've got an all new show.'

Miller liked Millie and was happy to tell her as he left that he'd love to see the new show. He felt sad to think of how quiet Millie's place had become and hoped the men were there just to have a good time. And it made him more determined to clean up Pecos.

He walked back over to Jim Wood's store and told him what he'd gleaned. He did go back to Millie's that evening. Cal Withers and his men were watching Millie's floor show. There weren't many people in the audience, just enough to make a go of things. Miller found Millie and commented on how quiet the place was.

'It ain't no wonder,' was Millie's reply. 'The way things is in this town. Those are your men over there,' she commented, knowing their presence was what he come in to enquire about.

She pointed out Cal Withers to him. He and his men were sitting at a couple of tables. It was obvious they were enjoying the show, though Withers was less enthusiastic about showing it than the others.

'Seems respectable-looking enough,' Miller remarked, obviously referring to Withers. 'What d'you suppose he and his men have come into town for?'

'Probably just passing through,' Millie replied.

'Maybe,' Miller said. 'Think I'll hang around a bit and see what, if anything, gives.'

'That's fine by me, Mitch,' Millie replied, then, with a smile adding, 'you know you're always welcome here. In fact, we don't see you nearly often enough.'

He smiled back and then wandered over to the bar to get himself a beer. He took it and sat down at a table next to Withers. Withers noticed his arrival but made nothing of it. He thought Miller looked a sober sort of person who didn't necessarily fit in with the surroundings but that was all. Then, as the moments went by, he noticed Miller looking at him. He began to wonder if Miller had somehow recognized him.

There was no sheriff's badge, he could see that, and Miller did not have the look of a bounty hunter about him. They were a very definite type and he could clearly see that Miller was not of the sort. Besides, he was too young-looking. So who was he and why did he keep looking over at him? It was making Withers feel so uneasy that he thought of asking Miller what he was looking at. But he knew better than to do that. He was here to do a job and didn't want to go making himself an object of people's attention.

Miller was having thoughts of his own. He'd come to the conclusion that Withers wasn't there because he'd been sent for. Norris and his like were lowlife opportunists; there was nothing lowlife about Withers. On the contrary, he had a distinguished look about him. His clothes were of good quality and were well cut. Maybe he was a rancher or something, simply passing through. Maybe he was looking to buy land. Who knows, Miller concluded, he could be in Pecos for any one of a hundred reasons.

He finished his drink and got up to leave. Millie's chorus girls were putting on a great show and the clientele, Withers' men amongst them, were lapping it up. As they all cheered and whistled, none of them paid Miller any attention as he got up to leave. Withers, though, did take notice. He fixed a stare on Miller and kept it on him as he made his way around the tables to leave. At one point Miller looked at him and their eyes met. Neither man gave anything of himself away and Miller simply passed on into the foyer of the hotel. There he met Millie.

'Leaving so soon?' she remarked to him.

'Yeah, well . . .' Miller said, not really having anything to say. He wasn't out for a good time and besides Hannah was at home waiting for him.

'D'you make anything of Withers. Cal Withers, that's his name?' Millie asked, knowing that Withers and not the show was the only reason for Miller's being there.

'Nah,' Miller replied. 'There don't seem to be much to make anything of. If there is, I guess we'll know soon enough.'

'Well, all right, then.' Millie smiled at him. Knowing he'd be going home to Hannah Voegel, she added: 'Say hello to Hannah for me. And you take care, Mitch. That was a brave thing you did facing down Norris the other day but we don't want you getting hurt.'

'Someone's gotta stand up to him,' Miller replied, taking his gun from the desk clerk, to whom he'd given it on entering the hotel.

'I know that, Mitch,' Millie replied. 'Just be careful, that's all I'm saying.'

Acknowledging her concerns with a smile, Miller took his leave.

Millie knew everything that went on in town but she kept it to herself. Much as she thought of herself as a lady, she knew that few other people in Pecos did. Especially amongst the respectable classes. Consequently she didn't mix much. She knew that plans were afoot to replace Sheriff Lock with Miller. Like many people she reckoned Miller was too young for the job but somehow she was beginning to get the feeling that he was growing into it. She smiled after him as he left, then turned to go back about her business in the hotel, where she bumped into Cal Withers. His men were still enjoying the floor show and consequently he was alone.

He and Millie didn't know one another but each of them recognized someone of stature in the other and so could accord one another a certain level of openness.

'Someone of importance around here?' Withers asked Millie, indicating with a turn of his head in the direction of the door that he was talking about Miller.

'Who, Mitch?' Millie replied, adding knowingly: 'No, no, at least not yet.'

But that was all she was going to say and Withers, sensing this, didn't enquire further. Instead, he turned, and, taking a short drag on a cigarillo he went back into the music hall.

EIGHT

It was still hot in Pecos but as the day wore on it began to look like rain. Over night a storm blew in. It brought with it rains such as Pecos hadn't seen in a long time and by the morning the town was awash. By midday Main Street had turned into a quagmire. People gave up trying to move about town and the Broken Spoke saloon became even fuller than normal of the lowlife that liked to gather there.

The rain suddenly fell more heavily than ever, drumming loudly on the roof of the saloon.

'When's it gonna stop?' a customer asked Zeb Turner, who was pouring the man a drink.

'Don't ask me,' was Turner's reply, 'I ain't looked at the sky for a while but it can't go on for ever.'

The customer wasn't anyone particularly well known to Turner and he didn't linger to let a conversation develop. As he turned away to drop into the till the cost of a beer his mind quickly turned to the scheduled town council meeting set for that afternoon. There was no guarantee it would now take place. The saloon was fairly humming and he could see that Norris was being swept along with it and getting very drunk. Looking at his fob-watch, Turner saw it was gone midday. He decided it'd be worthwhile talking to Norris. He wanted to make sure he was still feeling as murderous as he'd felt the day before.

He walked from behind the bar and pushed his way through the saloon to where Norris was sitting dealing hands. He whispered into Norris's right ear.

'We'd better talk,' he said.

Norris didn't seem to get the point. He looked up at Turner quizzically, then carried on dealing and barely took his eye off the pack.

'The rain,' Turner persevered. 'It might be just what we need.'

'Yeah,' Norris replied, though still not really getting the point. 'What time is it?' he asked, raising his voice to be heard over the din of the saloon.

Turner didn't need to get out his watch. Only a few minutes had passed since he had last done so.

'A quarter after noon. The council's gonna be meeting at two, don't forget.'

Norris won the hand he was playing and let out a triumphant remark. He had fleeced everyone at the table for the last couple of hours and the players were beginning to feel the pinch. They didn't stake fortunes but what they did stake was all they had. There was enough of it, however, to make a considerable pile in front of Norris. Half of it belonged to Turner. Normally anything that brought people into his saloon and kept them there was most welcome to Turner but today there was something more pressing to be dealt with.

Norris didn't seem to see the need to talk further and it irritated Turner.

'I said we need to talk,' he said again into Norris's right ear, this time in less of a whisper, as Norris began to deal another hand. Norris looked impatient.

'All right, all right,' he suddenly declared. He passed the deck of cards over to Ben Kirk, who was as usual at his side, and told him to deal.

He took off his hat and raked the bank into it, then got up and followed Turner to a room in the back of the saloon. A fiddler was giving a rough-sawn rendition of *Turkey in the Straw* and as Norris passed through the saloon he paused for a moment to tap a foot along with a dozen other jigging men and enjoy the music.

'Eee ha!' he sang out raucously, as he turned to follow Turner.

Other men, knowing who he was and holding him in fear and awe, echoed his cry in a false show of fellowship. He was humming along with the fiddler's playing as he stepped into the room and joined Turner. Turner shut the door behind him.

'Looks like you been doing well in there, Norris,' Turner remarked. 'The rain ain't everyone's enemy.'

'Is that what you brought me in here to say?' Norris asked impatiently.

'No, no,' Turner replied, 'You seem to have forgotten the problem we've got with Miller. We gotta do something about it and do it fast. There's gonna be a town council meeting this afternoon and they're aiming to take Lock's badge off of him and pin it on Miller.'

'Yeah?' Norris questioned him.

'Well, if it happens, you know what it's gonna mean for us?'

Turner said nothing more, waiting to see what Norris was going to say next. Norris, though, simply stood and looked at him. Seeing how drunk Norris was, Turner suddenly lost his patience. He came straight to the point.

'You gotta kill Miller, now, Norris,' he said. 'You just gotta do it. Now, before it's too late.'

Swaying a little, Norris gave him the drunkard's watery-eyed, unbothered stare.

'OK,' he said, enlightened at last. 'Trouble is he ain't been seen about much. Maybe he suddenly got wise about what's best for him and he's cleared out of town.'

'Get real, Norris,' Turner said impatiently. 'He's probably just sitting out the rain at Hannah Voegel's.'

'So what you want me to do, Zeb? Go kill him there?' Norris asked.

'Go kill him where you like. Just kill him, Norris. Before it's too late.'

Norris looked at him. In his drunkenness he was able to remember he'd been humiliated enough times at the hands of Miller. He wasn't, he reckoned, readily going to risk being humiliated by him again.

'I'll kill him,' he said, slurring his words, 'when I'm ready in my own sweet way, in my own sweet time.'

Turner could have cursed with frustration.

On the other side of Main Street, Jim Wood was looking out of the large window of his general stores. He'd seen heavy rain before but it felt to him as if he'd never seen rain like this. People had sunk up to their ankles in the mud and wagons and buggies had been abandoned, their horses unharnessed. Uppermost on his mind, too, was the question of whether or not the town council meeting could take place. He hadn't seen Miller since the day before and he guessed he was holed up somewhere waiting for the weather to clear. He was beginning to wonder again whether the town council would be able to hold its meeting, when he saw Dwight Cash, the blacksmith, coming striding across Main Street like an ox, the mud hardly bothering him, towards the store.

'Ain't it ever gonna stop?' Cash greeted him, as he came through the door of the store.

He was wearing a broad-brimmed Stetson and an oilskin as big as a tent. Both of them were dripping water.

'It doesn't look like it, does it?' was Wood's reply, as he stopped looking out of the window and took a few steps towards Cash.

If he'd stayed looking out of the window a second longer he'd have seen Zeb Turner step through the batwing doors of the saloon on to the plank-walk in front of it.

'We gonna go ahead with the meeting, Jim?' Cash asked him, as he took off his hat and oilskin and shook them.

'That's what I was wondering,' Wood remarked. 'Ain't seen anything of Miller, have you?'

'No, I ain't. Saw Lock sitting in his office as I came past, but that's about all.'

Wood pulled out his fob-watch from a pocket in his waistcoat.

'It's a half after one,' he informed the blacksmith.

'Feels like this town has got a curse on it. Much more rain like this and the whole place will just float on down into the river.'

'Maybe,' Wood said, distracted.

There was coffee on a stove and he offered some to Cash.

Back in the Broken Spoke saloon Norris was again at his card-table dealing crooked hands to unsuspecting cowpokes. Turner had decided he needed to go take a look outside at the weather. He looked up into the sky and came to the conclusion that the rain wasn't going to last much longer, so he took the notion to go and see if Lock was in his office. He found him sitting at his desk. Both men greeted one another.

'Looks like the rain is gonna buy us some time,' Lock remarked.

'Time for what?' Turner asked.

'Just time, I guess,' Lock replied, sitting back in his seat and putting his hands behind his head.

'Seen any more of Miller?' Turner asked pointedly.

'Nope,' Lock replied, shrugging his shoulders. 'Reckon he's just waiting to be appointed sheriff and then he'll make his move.'

'That's what I've been telling Norris but he don't seem to feel there's any urgency in the matter.'

'Maybe he's right. What else can we do but bide our time until he makes a move?' Lock asked.

Turner hadn't really expected Lock to make any other kind of reply. The man was a coward and it showed in everything he did. This was just another example of it.

'Well,' he replied impatiently, 'I was just telling Norris I didn't think we could afford to wait for Miller to make his next move. That we ought to kill him now, before the town council gets the chance to pin a badge on him.'

'If I arrest him, he won't be able to make a next move,' Lock remarked lamely.

'*If* you arrest him,' Turner felt like saying in

mockery to Lock but he thought better of it. Instead he said: 'Look, if you can find out where Miller is, Norris will finish him off. Then we can all sit back and relax.'

Lock didn't say anything in reply. He just stared at Turner.

'Well?' Turner asked, wanting to elicit some sort of reply from Lock. His tone of voice was beginning to show impatience.

NINE

Jim Wood looked out of the window of his general store to see what the weather was looking like.

'Guess we should make our way over to the town hall and see what gives,' Dwight Cash remarked to him.

'Skies are suddenly looking clearer,' Wood said. 'Happen it's gonna stop raining soon.'

'You're right,' Cash agreed, going and standing by Wood to look out of the window.

They both saw Sheriff Lock step out of his office on to the plank-walk followed closely by Zeb Turner.

'What's Zeb doing with Lock?' Cash asked.

'Search me,' Wood replied. 'Cooking up

something, no doubt. Perhaps they was both hoping the rain was gonna stop the council meeting. They both gotta a lot to lose by Lock losing his badge.'

'This meeting or another, I can't see what difference it makes,' Cash said. 'He's gonna lose his badge or this town is gonna lose its blacksmith.'

Jim Wood turned to look at Cash. He knew he was serious. He had a wife and six children and had been saying for a long time now that Pecos was no longer the place any respectable man would want to raise a family.

'He's going, Dwight, you don't have to worry about that. He's going,' Wood reassured him, pulling out his fob watch in time to see the minute hand move on to the fifty-minute mark. 'Come on,' he added. 'Time we was in the town hall.'

As the men stepped out of Wood's store, they came level with Sheriff Lock and Zeb Turner on the other side of Main Street. It was still raining, though not as hard. Both pairs of men stopped and stared at one another. The air between them became tense with loathing, as each pair had their own thoughts about the other. Lock in his blindly cowardly way was determined that by the end of the day he'd still be sheriff of Pecos. While Wood and Cash were equally determined that he should not. Turner's only concerns lay in safeguarding business, his own.

As the two pairs of men stood eyeballing one another, they could hear the sound of revelling coming from the Broken Spoke saloon. The fiddle continued to squeal and feet were still stamping out the beat on the saloon's puncheon floor. Turner and Lock couldn't help but be mindful of the high profits it would be earning them. Then suddenly a shot rang out. The fiddling stopped and the wood beneath their feet suddenly became still. Each man looked at the other. Then they turned to look in the direction of the saloon's batwing doors. As they did so another shot rang out. And then another.

'Sounds like trouble to me,' Jim Wood called out to Lock pointedly. 'Ain't you gonna do something about it?'

Lock made no reply.

'Thought not,' Cash said loudly enough for Lock and Turner to hear.

Then he and Wood continued their interrupted walk to the town hall. As they did so, Turner, followed by Lock, stepped into the Broken Spoke. They found what they expected. Turner hurried to get behind the bar. He didn't wear a sidearm and wanted to get to his shotgun. Sheriff Lock, though, did wear a weapon and he had it drawn as he pushed his way through the crowd to get to where he knew Norris would be. Normally he would have turned and walked away from any trouble that was going on in the saloon, leaving it to Norris and Ben Kirk to resolve as they would, which meant in their own bloody but victorious way. But with Jim Wood and Dwight Cash watching, he knew he had at the very least to be seen to be doing something about it.

'Stand back, stand back!' he snapped, as he pushed his way through the drunken clientele of the saloon.

The sight that greeted him was not a happy one. If Norris and Kirk were in control of the situation, the hold they had on it was only tenuous and it looked as if they might lose it at any moment.

Kirk and Norris were standing on one side

of the gambling table with their guns drawn and their chairs kicked over behind them. On the other were three tough looking cowpokes with their guns drawn and cocked. All of them had their shooting arms outstretched, their guns levelled at one anothers' chests. Lying over the table was a corpse. Slumped in a chair was another. The saloon was as quiet as a graveside gathering.

'All right, all right,' Lock suddenly declared, reckoning it was safe to try and take command of the situation. 'Let's just calm things down here.'

'Don't interfere, Matt,' Norris advised him through gritted teeth, 'in what don't concern you.'

He was very drunk, his gun hand shaking visibly, but Lock knew he was in control of himself.

'I'm the sheriff, Norris,' Lock replied, 'which means it does concern me.'

Turning to look at him, Norris gave him that kind of look that asked 'so what?'

'He was cheating,' one of the cowpokes informed Lock, as if it was all that needed to be said.

Norris raised his gun threateningly, as if to tell the cowpoke that if he said it one more time he'd pay the price. The cowpoke in turn raised his gun and stretched his arm out even further.

Lock was confused. He could see that neither side was minded to back down. To gain control of the situation, he'd have to get tough in a way he didn't really know how. Everyone in the saloon knew it and looked on eagerly to see what would happen next. The stand-off continued, with neither side minded to back down. It was not a situation Norris was used to but he was drunk and the more drunk he was the meaner he got.

From behind the bar, Turner could see the kind of trouble that was looming and he had no faith in Lock's ability to get the better of it. He decided he'd have to help him out. He grabbed his shotgun from the under the bar and pushed his way through the still silent crowd of less than sober cowpokes to where the trouble was. As he got there, he made his presence known to them all by cocking the two hammers of his sawed-off American Arms 12-gauge shotgun.

'You heard what the sheriff said,' he snarled between gritted teeth, 'let's cool this thing down some.'

Kirk and the card-players, realizing their disadvantaged position, might have listened, but Norris, as ever the irascible, bullying thug, would not.

'Nobody calls me a cheat and lives to repeat it,' he said.

'Norris, I said we're gonna cool it here,' Turner repeated. 'Now let's just all slowly put our guns down.'

'You heard him,' Lock, not wanting to be edged out of any solution to the problem, interjected. 'Now, all of you just lower your guns.'

While Norris's eyes remained fixed on the man whose chest his gun was levelled at, the eyes of the card-players darted from Lock to Turner and back to Norris and Kirk. Their desire was to do what they were told and then to back out of a situation they knew they couldn't any longer win.

'You heard the sheriff. Now back off, all of you,' Turner said, as if reading their minds.

Norris, making it look as if he was at last

going to comply with Turner's and Lock's demands, lowered his gun. The others followed suit. Then, in a swift about face, he raised his gun again and shot the card-player in front of him. As the other two card-players quickly turned their guns in his direction, beginning to squeeze their triggers, Turner and Lock turned theirs on them. The two cowpokes didn't know what hit them. It was a fierce storm of lead issuing from four weapons: Norris's, Kirk's, Lock's and Turner's. They didn't stand a chance.

'I said,' Norris declared, as the thunder of gunfire gave way to silence, 'no one calls me a cheat and lives to repeat it.'

Nobody else said anything. They stood in stunned silence as the smell of cordite filled their nostrils, reminding them who ruled in Pecos town.

TEN

Cal Withers, the leader of the six riders, had stepped out on to the plank-walk outside Millie's Hotel when the last bout of gun firing had started in the Broken Spoke saloon. It was still raining and a wind was blowing up Main Street. It carried the sound of gunfire from the saloon to Withers' ears. He was thinking of how the town was living up to its reputation, when he was joined by one of his long riders, Bill Coral, who was his number two.

'Rain seems to be easing off some, Cal,' Bill Coral said to him. 'Maybe the time's right to do it.'

'I don't think so, Bill,' was Withers' reply.

'The ground's still too wet. It's a quagmire and would seriously hinder our getaway. I don't think we can take the chance.'

Bill Coral looked out from the plank-walk at the skies above Pecos.

'Guess you're right,' he agreed with Withers. 'Ain't no hurry. It can wait, I guess.'

'Why don't we go check out the saloon,' Withers remarked, indicating with a tilt of his head the Broken Spoke.

'Yeah, why don't we,' Coral replied. 'I'll get the others. They're beginning to get a mite bored hanging out here. Seems they might like there to be a bit more of their kind of fun.'

'Yeah,' was all Withers said in reply.

Then the two turned round and walked back into Millie's Hotel.

They were seen by Miller, who, taking advantage of a break in the weather, was walking up Main Street. He guessed who they were and wondered again what they were doing in town. He had no time to investigate now, however. The meeting of the town council was scheduled to take place shortly and he guessed that with the rain having practically stopped it would go ahead as planned. No one had said different, but sitting in Hannah's for most of the morning keeping out of the rain he had begun to wonder.

As he approach the town hall he came across Jim Wood and Dwight Cash. He and they greeted one another.

'Looks like the rain's let up just in time,' Miller remarked, looking out from the plank-walk on to Main Street.

'Sure does,' Dwight Cash agreed.

'You hear all that sound of shooting coming from inside the Broken Spoke?' Jim Wood asked Miller.

'Ain't nothing new,' Miller remarked.

'No,' replied Wood, 'but Dwight and I were just wondering if someone has saved us the bother of sacking Lock.'

'I doubt if he was on the receiving end of any of it,' Wood replied. 'He's too clever for that. The man don't ever knowingly put himself in the way of danger.'

'Well, I suppose we'll find out soon enough,' Miller remarked.

They stepped off the end of one plank-walk, squelched through water and mud and climbed up on to another that lead to the town hall.

'Ain't no reason not to have a meeting now,' Wood remarked, looking at the weather.

'So long as everyone's in town,' Cash replied.

Wood agreed with him. He and Cash were the first of the town council members to step into the town hall.

'Looks like we're the first to arrive,' Wood remarked to Cash.

Just as Wood said it, the town baker, Hal Wade, stepped into the hall.

'Hal,' Cash greeted him, 'we was just beginning to wonder if there was gonna be a meeting at all.'

Hal Wade was of Dutch extraction and looked every bit the part, with a round, chubby face, round wire spectacles and a full drooping moustache.

'Well, I'm here and I think the others are on their way. D'you hear all that noise coming from the Broken Spoke?' he asked.

'Sure did and we was wondering if maybe someone had saved us the bother of sacking Sheriff Lock,' replied Wood.

'Afraid not. I just saw him coming out of the saloon. Five bodies were thrown out into the mud ahead of him, none of which I recognized.'

Wood and Cash looked at one another and raised their eyebrows. Just then another three men came into the hall. One of them was the town undertaker. It might have been said that he was the only person who benefited from the lack of law and order in Pecos, but in fact this was not the case. Most of the dead, especially those without any real connections in the town, were simply thrown into the Pecos River. There were just too many of them and the citizens of Pecos had no interest in bearing the cost of their disposal.

'So we can be expecting a visit from him,' Wood said, while acknowledging with a nod of the head the others as they arrived.

Soon all the members were assembled and the meeting was convened and brought to order by the town council chairman, Tom Cowell.

'Well, gentlemen,' he said, 'We all know why we're here.'

But before he could say any more Sheriff

Matt Lock suddenly appeared, walking in through the door.

Lock's sudden appearance took everyone by surprise and it was greeted with what for Lock was an uncomfortable silence. Sensing this and reckoning it was to his advantage Lock stepped up to where the councillors were all seated at a long, rectangular table. He spoke in strident tones.

'You asked for my presence at today's meeting,' he observed. 'So here I am. I hope I ain't kept you gentlemen waiting, but as I am sure you must all know by now, it's been a busy afternoon for me so far.'

Stunned by his effrontery, the councillors remained silent and staring at him. The only man who wasn't thrown by Lock's behaviour was Tom Cowell. He was, after all, a lawyer and trained not to be fooled by appearances.

'Quite so,' was his reply to Lock's statement. 'But I hope you didn't rush anything for our benefit, Matt. The rain's rather delayed the opening of this meeting and we ain't exactly ready for you yet. Perhaps you could come back later.'

Lock didn't seem to want to agree to what

had been suggested. He'd noticed Miller's presence.

'Is there something wrong with that?' Tom Cowell asked him at last, seeing just how perturbed Lock looked at the suggestion of going away and coming back later.

'Well, there is really,' Lock replied falteringly. Then, turning on Miller, he suddenly declared, 'Miller, you're under arrest.'

The whole gathering looked upon Lock, stunned. There was a long silence. Then Tom Cowell spoke.

'Matt, in case you didn't hear, we said we were *not* ready for you yet.'

Lock knew what was being said to him. He didn't have the character to stand up to the likes of Tom Cowell. He knew he'd only make a fool of himself if he insisted on trying to arrest Miller. But he felt he had to persist.

'Tom, I am the sheriff of this town. You all appointed me and I've got good reason for arresting Miller here. He's breaking the law even now,' he said, noticing that Miller was wearing his gun. 'I wouldn't be doing my job if I didn't arrest him.'

Miller's hand went to his gun but otherwise

he showed no reaction. He was too busy trying to anticipate Tom Cowell's reaction to what Lock had said.

Tom Cowell's reaction was to ignore every word of it.

'Let me repeat what I said, Matt,' he said, 'in case you didn't get my drift. We aren't ready for you yet. Now have you got a problem with that?'

Lock began to squirm. None of the people around the table liked him and they were all glad to see it. Lock couldn't help but see it. And if he hadn't known it before, he knew it now, the game was indeed up. Without saying another word to the councillors or Miller, he turned and slowly walked out of the town hall. Standing on the steps of the plank-walk outside he pondered what to do next. He decided to go to the Broken Spoke saloon. He had to see Turner.

He found him in his usual place behind the bar. Pushing through the crowd of revellers, he went up to him.

'You still sheriff?' Turner asked him.

He could see that Lock was still wearing his badge.

'The town council told me they weren't ready for me. They told me to come back later.'

'Was Miller there?' Turner asked.

'He was,' Lock replied, 'but when I tried to arrest him they showed nothing but contempt for me.'

'And you let 'em?' Turner asked scornfully.

'Well, what else was I supposed to do? They're the town council, ain't they?'

Turner said nothing in reply. He had no need to. His look said it all.

'What we gonna do?' Lock asked him.

'It's a bit late for that, don't you think?' Turner replied.

'I thought you said if I found Miller, Norris would finish him off.'

'I did,' Turner replied.

'Well, ain't you gonna go and tell him Miller's in the town hall?' Lock asked earnestly.

'Why don't you? Turner asked in turn.

Lock didn't have a reply for him. He just turned his head and looked in Norris's direction.

'Guess he'll find out soon enough,' he remarked to Turner.

Turner threw him a look of contempt.

'And when he does,' he said in reply, 'best you ain't nowhere around.'

Turner's words made Lock look fit to fill his pants. Without waiting to hear any more, he suddenly turned and left the Broken Spoke in a hurry. Turner's curses went with him.

ELEVEN

Cal Withers and his men strolled into the Broken Spoke saloon. Things had quietened down a bit and Sheriff Matt Lock, for sheriff he still was, was standing by the bar finishing a drink. Norris was at his card table and there was a quiet hum filling the place. When Withers and his men entered the saloon they came to a halt just inside the batwing doors while Withers surveyed the place. As he stood there looking around heads began to turn towards him and slowly the place became quiet.

Withers was a distinguished looking six footer who had an air of authority about him. It seemed to Lock, Turner and everyone else that he'd come into the saloon for a reason and they began to wonder what it was. Less than a minute passed before Withers led his men to the bar.

'Sheriff,' he said cordially to Lock as he came to a halt beside him.

Lock, looking uneasy, returned the greeting with a tilt of his head and stood by to let Withers get closer to the bar.

'Whiskey for me and beer for my men,' was all Withers said by way of a greeting to Turner, who rushed to get a new bottle of redeye and a shot-glass to put in front him.

Withers was aware of the effect he'd had on everyone gathered in the Broken Spoke and he began to sense that he might be intruding on something. While Turner filled beer glasses for Withers' men, Withers, having filled his shot glass with redeye, turned around once again to cast his eye about the place.

'Seems like there was a spot of bother round here today,' he remarked to Lock.

Lock didn't immediately find words to reply to Withers. Seeing this, Turner jumped in and made a reply for him.

'It was nothing out of the ordinary. Just a

bunch of bad losers who accused Norris over there of cheating.'

Withers looked over to where Norris was sitting dealing cards to a number of players seated around his table.

'Is that right?' Withers asked.

'Yeah,' Turner replied. 'Sheriff Lock here intervened and the matter got sorted out.'

Withers looked at Lock. Withers had had his share of dealings with lawmen and Lock didn't appear to him to be capable of sorting anything out.

'Is that right, Sheriff?' Withers asked Lock.

Lock shook his head uncertainly and muttered: 'Sure is.'

'You the gambling sort?' Turner ventured to ask Withers, hoping he'd made it sound like a casual enquiry.

Withers simply smiled ironically in reply. Then he wandered over to where Norris was sitting playing cards.

In the town hall Tom Cowell and his fellow councillors were discussing with Miller why he thought he might be a suitable replacement for Lock.

'He didn't do so badly in disarming Norris and Kirk when they murdered that card-player they chased out of the Broken Spoke on to Main Street,' Jim Wood had commented.

'Yes,' agreed Dwight Cash, 'if he'd had the powers of the town sheriff then, those two men would have been put behind bars and would be on their way to doing time in the State Penitentiary.'

Everyone agreed. The matter of advertising for a new sheriff was touched upon, but it was agreed that there was no time for that.

'Look,' insisted Jim Wood, 'Miller here has shown he has the backbone for the job and I put forward the motion that we appoint Miller as town sheriff. Let's put it to the vote.'

'But what about this nonsense of Lock's regarding his intention of arresting Miller?' Cowell asked.

Ever the lawyer, he had to make sure they didn't leave themselves exposed to criticism.

'His argument is that Miller broke the law: firstly, by wearing a gun in town, and secondly, by shooting at Norris and the other man before they shot at him,' Wood commented.

'Yet he's never arrested anyone else for these offences, which are committed day in day out, I know,' Cowell replied.

'Exactly who is in charge of this town?' one of the other councillors asked.

'Well, I guess we, the town council, are,' Tom Cowell answered.

'Good!' the councillor declared, 'It was just that I was beginning to wonder.'

'Well,' said another, 'if that is the case, let's do as Jim here suggested and put it to the vote.'

Tom Cowell agreed. He called for a show of hands in support of the motion and it was passed unanimously.

'Right,' declared Tom Cowell. 'Looks like we oughta send for Lock then, and tell him.'

'You won't regret it,' Miller remarked.

'That's in your hands now, Miller,' Tom Cowell replied, 'but by all accounts we won't.'

Lock was sent for and told he was being given the sack.

'I hate to have to say this to you, Matt, but it's the unanimous decision of this meeting to fire you. You ain't done your job and the law and order situation in this town has gone from bad to worse under your tenure of office.'

Sheriff Lock could not pretend to look shocked at what he was told and only made a weak attempt to defend himself.

'I tried my best, Tom, but this town is uncontrollable,' he said, not focusing his eyes on Cowell or any of the members of the council. 'You'd need an army to clean it up.'

'If you needed help, you'd only to ask for it,' Cowell replied. 'And as for arresting Miller here, do you really think it'd be the appropriate thing to do, under the circumstances?'

Lock didn't have anything to say in reply. There was a few moments' silence as everyone's eyes turned first to Lock and then from him to Miller. Lock felt the weight of the silence bear down upon him. It seemed to be accusing him of what he knew he was guilty of and he thought he would break under the strain of it.

'What's more, Matt, you've colluded with the bad elements in this town,' Tom Cowell said, breaking the silence at last. 'And you made the situation worse than it was when you pinned on that badge,' he continued, indicating with a pointing index finger that he was talking about the sheriff's badge that was pinned on Lock's chest. 'You took an oath, Matt, but you didn't honour it.'

Lock involuntarily fingered the badge. Cowell and the rest of the committee waited for him to make a reply but he didn't. He knew that what he was being accused of was true but he didn't have the guts to put up even the pretence of a defence. Instead his thoughts quickly went to how much money Turner had corruptly paid him to keep his nose out of the Broken Spoke's business, wondering how far it would take him in realizing his ambitions.

His silence spoke volumes to the men he was standing before and their contempt for him grew even greater. They all wondered how they'd ever been stupid enough to appoint him sheriff in the first place. Then they remembered how desperate they'd been at the time for someone, anyone, to take on the job. Well, they weren't desperate any more and their contempt for him knew no bounds.

It was obvious to Cowell by now that Lock was not going to say anything to defend his reputation.

'All right,' he said. 'Give us the badge, Matt.'

Lock's fingers went quickly to undo it. As he took it off and stepped forward to put it on the table at which the councillors sat, Cowell said:

'We ought to be ordering your arrest on charges of corruption and failure to do your duty but instead we're gonna run you out of town. You've got till dawn. If you're still here then, you will be arrested.'

Lock was visibly shaken by what Cowell had said to him. Beads of sweat formed on his brow. But there was worse to come. Cowell hadn't finished.

'But before you leave, Matt, you can deposit with Reverend Tapper a donation to the fund for the rebuilding of the church. And make sure it's a generous one.'

A look of confusion spread across Lock's face. He knew that if he wanted to save his skin he had no choice but to comply with Cowell's orders. Everyone's eyes were upon him and he couldn't have felt more humiliated and brought down. All he wanted now was to get away from their presence.

'Whatever you say, Tom,' were the only

words he muttered before turning and walking out of the town hall.

Once he'd gone, Miller was handed the
badge to pin on to the left-hand breast of his
waistcoat. Then he swore an oath and having
done so felt ready for business.

'Only thing I need now is deputies,' he
announced to the town councillors.

The town councillors all looked to one
another but none of them had an answer to
give to him.

TWELVE

Lock didn't waste any time in letting Turner and the others know that he had been sacked.

'It's about what was expected,' was Turner's cutting response. 'Question is: what we gonna do about it?'

As he spoke Turner's eyes turned in the direction of where Norris was playing cards. Seated opposite him was Cal Withers. Withers' men were standing around the table watching him play. Lock's eyes did not follow Turner's. He was too keen to get over to Turner exactly how complete his humiliation at the hands of the town council had been.

'They've given me till dawn to get out of town,' he added, 'and, what's more, are expecting me to make a big donation to the church rebuilding fund. Well, they can go sing for that!'

Turner wasn't listening. His mind was concentrated on other things. He was wondering whether the stranger and those who were obviously his men could be approached to join their side. They looked the rough and ready sort, despite Withers' distinguished appearance, whom money could buy.

'Zeb,' Lock asked impatiently, 'are you listening to me?'

'Yeah, yeah,' Turner replied distractedly. 'They can sing for your donation, you said.'

Turner's apparent lack of interest in Lock's predicament began to make Lock feel bitter.

'Ain't you gonna help me?' he asked Turner.

'Possibly,' Turner mused. 'Make it look as if you're fixing to do what they ask and come back later.'

Lock stared at Turner wondering why it was his mind seemed to be elsewhere. Turning to look in the direction where Turner's eyes were fixed, he saw the stranger who was sitting opposite Norris and the others who were standing around the table.

He didn't guess what Turner was thinking, just that for some reason or other they'd caught his attention. He noticed also that Norris wasn't looking his usual confident self as he dealt the cards.

'Norris losing or something?' he asked.

'What?' Turner replied, though still preoccupied with his own thoughts.

'I asked,' Lock began again, then, becoming even more impatient at Turner's seeming lack of interest in him, he snapped: 'never mind.'

Then he turned and walked out of the saloon. Turner's head turned momentarily to watch him go. He cursed him for being useless and then returned to his own thoughts. He wondered how it would be best to approach Withers and how much it would cost to hire him and his men.

Just at that moment it suddenly looked as if all hell was going to break loose at the card-table.

'I saw that,' one of Withers men, a fearless-looking cowpoke called Bartlett, suddenly declared.

Norris, who'd been dealing a crooked hand, suddenly froze. Then he looked up from the cards he'd been placing in front of himself and looked Withers in the eye.

'Saw what?' he asked of Bartlett, without turning to look at him.

'You pulled that ace from your sleeve.'

Norris barely showed any reaction. They were playing five card stud and he had dealt himself three aces and then a fourth. He'd dealt Withers a nine, a ten, a jack, a queen and a king, all of clubs. A royal flush is normally hard to beat. But a run of four aces is a hand that can do it. It was not likely that Lady Luck would have looked down so sweetly on both players. She hadn't, as Bartlett had seen.

'You calling me a cheat?' Norris asked him.

Turner saw what was going down at Norris's table and rushed to intervene.

'That's precisely what I'm calling you,' Bartlett sang out in menacing tones.

Withers saw Turner hurrying towards them. Norris, who had his back to Turner, didn't. He went to draw but wasn't quick enough. Withers, who'd said nothing so far, and his men were quicker and Turner arrived at the table to be greeted by seven drawn and cocked Colt .44s. There was a tense silence as all concerned waited to see what was going to happen next.

'Drop it,' Withers, breaking the silence, suddenly ordered Norris.

Norris eyeballed him. He was not used to being bested and particularly not in the Broken Spoke saloon. Other people in the saloon, especially those who'd been robbed at cards before by Norris, looked on, enjoying every second of what was beginning to look like his comeuppance. Norris, though, didn't look as if he was about to comply with Withers' command.

'Drop it, I said,' Withers repeated.

Ben Kirk, who had, as always, been sitting at Norris's side, had not drawn his gun when the others had. But now he was beginning to think he had to do something to come to Norris's aid. His shooting hand was beneath the table. It was still wrapped in bandages but he decided he was going to have to use it, if Norris was to stand any chance of not being gunned down. Slowly he began to move his hand towards his gun.

'No one calls me a cheat and lives to tell the

tale,' Norris, trotting out his old line of defence, replied to Withers.

'There must be some mistake,' Turner interjected, hoping to take the heat out of the situation.

'There ain't no mistake,' Bartlett informed Turner. 'I saw it clear as day. He pulled a card from up his sleeve.'

While everyone was seemingly distracted, Kirk thought he saw his chance and went for his gun. Seven men saw him do so and seven bullets riddled his chest. He was dead before Norris or Turner realized what had happened. Even before he hit the ground, thrown from the chair he'd been seated in, Withers and his men had turned their guns to point again at Norris.

'Now,' said Withers. 'You gonna drop it or what?'

Norris slowly leaned forward to place his gun on the card table in front of him. Turner wanted to say something in another attempt to take the heat out of the situation but couldn't think of anything to say.

At about the same time that Kirk was shot,

Miller was leaving the town hall, having been sworn in as Pecos town's new sheriff. He was barely through the door, which was still open behind him, when the seven gun shots that killed Ben Kirk were fired. He heard them and knew instantly where they came from. He turned around to look back into the room to see if the others had heard it, and thought again that what he needed was deputies. The others had indeed heard the shots, as had everyone in town.

'It's up to you now,' Jim Wood said to him. 'You're wearing the badge, Mitch. It's up to you. Good luck.'

None of the other councillors spoke. They simply looked at Miller, hoping to see in his face the confidence in his ability to do the job they'd seen only a few minutes before. He didn't disappoint them.

THIRTEEN

Miller could guess what was going down in the Broken Spoke. He even expected any minute to see one or more dead bodies being thrown out of the saloon on to Main Street. Instead he was surprised to see Cal Withers and his men step through the batwings on to the plank-walk outside the saloon. They looked up and down Main Street and then strode off in the direction of Millie's. Miller stood and watched them for a second or two and then thought he'd step into the Broken Spoke himself to see what indeed the gun shots had been about. He guessed that by now Lock would have told Turner and the others that he'd been stripped of his badge and that it had been pinned on him. Maybe they were expecting him to come and see what the shooting was about. If he did what they expected of him he'd be able to gauge what their reaction to him was going to be like. He was still expecting, though, before he got to Broken Spoke to see a body or bodies be thrown out of the saloon on to Main Street.

But nothing happened. He stepped into the saloon just as it was beginning to return to normal. But that return to normality was stopped by his entrance. Turner was still standing by Norris who was sitting back in his seat at the card table. Miller didn't at first see the dead body of Ben Kirk lying on the floor on the other side of the table. The lack of any obvious signs of trouble made Miller wonder if he'd been mistaken in thinking that the shots he'd heard earlier had come from the saloon.

The saloon had gone quiet when Miller had walked in through the batwings. Everyone had noticed the badge pinned on his chest and those who didn't already know guessed what it meant.

'I thought I heard gun shots come from here,' Miller said to Turner.

Turner didn't answer at first, instead looking at Norris. After a few seconds Miller repeated what he said.

Norris was so still that Miller wondered whether he was really alive. Maybe it was he who'd been shot. Turner suddenly spoke.

'Guess you did. Kirk's dead.'

As he spoke he indicated with a tilt of his head where Kirk was lying. Miller stepped closer in order to see Kirk's body.

'You just missed the men who did it,' Turner remarked. 'There were seven of them. Strangers in town. One of them was playing cards with Norris here and Kirk spotted him cheating. When he challenged him the man up and shot Kirk.'

Everyone in the saloon knew Turner was lying but nobody said anything. Despite his humiliation, the second time in one day, Norris remained in their eyes a formidable figure. They couldn't believe yet that even his number was up.

Miller walked around the table to get a better look at Kirk's body.

'Seems like he emptied his gun into him,' Miller remarked, noticing that Kirk's chest was riddled with bullet holes.

'It wasn't just him, they all took a shot at him,' Turner remarked.

'And you let them get away with it?' Miller asked Norris.

'There were too many of them,' Turner informed Miller before Norris could reply.

Miller had never seen Norris so cowed and guessed there was something more to the tale than he was being told.

'Is that right, Norris? Too many even for you?' Miller asked.

He noticed that there was no money on the table. Usually there was a pile of it and all of it belonging to Norris. Miller guessed that somehow or other Norris had been humili-ated by Cal Withers.

'You telling me, Norris, that not only did they shoot Kirk but that they stole the bank too?'

This was too much for Norris, who was by now beginning to recover himself. He had a reputation to maintain and by God he was going to maintain it. He had noticed that Miller was wearing Lock's badge and he was expecting trouble, more trouble, but of a kind he was sure he could deal with. He had to deal with it, if he was to salvage anything of his tarnished reputation. He suddenly stood up.

'And what are you fixing to do about it?' he snapped at Miller, adding, 'Sheriff.'

'Well, usually,' Miller replied, looking Norris straight in the eye, 'when someone's been shot around here in the past it's been claimed as self-defence.'

'Well, this time it wasn't,' Norris snarled at him between gritted teeth, 'and there are enough witnesses to prove it.'

The 'witnesses' all looked at Norris in confusion. He was lying but they all knew why. They had watched Cal Withers come close to putting a bullet in his head. They had seen him turn from his usual brash, bullying self into a cowed wreck. But what was more, they'd seen him hand over hundreds of dollars to Cal Withers to buy off that bullet, the one that would have seen him follow hot on the heels of Ben Kirk to wherever it was bad men like him and Kirk went when they left this world to inhabit the next.

'Hmm,' was the only sound Miller made in

reply to what Norris had said.

'Well, don't just stand there,' Norris snarled at him. 'Get out there and get after them. You're the sheriff now, ain't you? Or ain't you got the spunk for dealing with real murder?'

Miller was too cool-headed to allow himself to be baited by Norris.

'Better get the undertaker for Kirk,' he said to Turner.

Then he turned and walked away as if he was going to leave the saloon.

'They're gonna pay,' Norris suddenly declared, spitting the words after Miller. 'And if you don't make them, I will.'

It was obvious to everyone what he was talking about. Miller stopped and turned around.

'There's a lot that's got to be paid for around here,' he said, pointedly looking first at Norris and then at Turner. 'And I'll be coming back to collect.'

Both Norris and Turner knew what he was referring to but neither of them showed it. Turner simply turned away and walked back to the bar, while Norris merely eyeballed Miller in a defiant way. His gun was lying on the table in front of him. He wouldn't have used it, though, had it been sitting conveniently in its holster. He didn't want to risk being humiliated again in front of the very people before whom he needed to appear murderously mean. Miller could see this. Satisfied that he'd done enough to show that things had changed in Pecos, he turned and finished taking his leave of the Broken Spoke saloon.

FOURTEEN

Sheriff Mitch Miller had made his mark on the Broken Spoke saloon. Now he had to go and put his imprint on his office. He hoped Lock had vacated it by now.

As he stepped across Main Street this was not the only thing he had on his mind. The reality was that now he was the law in Pecos. But he was alone. He needed deputies and he could think of no one to pin a badge on. There was always Dwight Cash, but he had a wife and a large family and Miller didn't think it was fair to ask him to put his life on the line for the town and risk leaving his wife a widow and his children fatherless.

He had thought of Cal Withers and his men, even if only as a temporary measure.

But now they were implicated in the shooting dead of Ben Kirk he didn't know whether he should be thinking of them. Except that they had obviously bested Norris, which had to be a mark in their favour. Maybe they could be counted upon simply to frighten Norris into getting out of town. He didn't know and wouldn't know until he had presented himself to Cal Withers as sheriff and heard what his version of events was.

Having crossed Main Street he stepped on to the plank-walk adjacent to the sheriff's office. As he put his handle on the office door it became apparent to him that Lock was still in there. He was studying one of a pile of Wanted notices he had in front of him. Also on the desk was a wooden box into which he had obviously been putting his things. Miller guessed it might be tactless presenting himself so soon, but it was too late. Lock had already seen him.

'Matt,' Miller greeted him, casually enough, he hoped, as he stepped in through the opened door.

Lock simply threw him a look of contempt and carried on studying the Wanted notice he had in his hands. Miller was prepared to be gentlemanly about what had happened but it didn't look as if he was going to be given the chance.

'Got what you wanted, then?' Lock remarked to him, looking up.

'What I want,' Miller replied, 'is a cleaned up town.'

'And you think you're the man to do it?' Lock asked sneeringly.

'Look, Matt, what's happened has happened. You had your chance and you blew it. That's all there is to it. Now it's someone else's turn,' Miller replied.

'Maybe, if you think you're gonna fare any better with Norris and Turner. Good luck to you, 'cause you're gonna need it.'

Miller could see that Lock was making an attempt to justify himself and he decided he was not going to be drawn into it.

'That's as maybe,' he said instead, 'but this is my office now and if you've collected what's yours . . .'

'Think I have,' Lock replied, seeming to take one last look at the face on the Wanted notice he was handling.

He put the notice back with the others and, taking his wooden box in hand, bustled out of the place. Miller felt like reminding him not to forget to make his donation to the church rebuilding fund before he left town, but didn't. His mind was quickly turning to more important matters. Like the fact that he was going to have to confront Cal Withers. 'When?' was on his mind. 'Now' the answer inescapably came back.

Looking about his office and observing the pile of Wanted notices that Lock had left scattered on the desk, he thought he'd bring in some of his own things to make it more his own later. There were a number of rifles in a cabinet on the wall behind the desk. They were locked in place by a padlocked metal chain. There was a bunch of keys on the desk on top of the Wanted papers. Miller guessed one of them would be the key to the cabinet. He was going to see Cal Withers and wondered whether he should take a rifle with him. Deciding against it, he picked up the bunch of keys and put them in a drawer. Then he collected together the Wanted notices and put them in another drawer. He had not yet come face to face with Cal Withers, but had he done so he'd have known that the face on the Wanted notice that Lock had been studying was that of Withers.

He finished what little tidying up he'd begun. The office now felt his. He looked about the room once more, fingered his sheriff's badge, then turned and left. He was going, as he knew he had to, to Millie's Hotel.

In Millie's Hotel Cal Withers and his men were getting ready to do what they'd come to Pecos to do. The afternoon was passing by and soon the bank would be closed. Millie had told Withers about the town's law and order problems and he had quietly smiled to himself. Millie had said for all the good the sheriff was to them they might as well not have had one. This was music to Withers' ears. It seemed to him that robbing the bank was going to be as easy as throwing a two-day calf. Proof of this had come in the fact that no one had come looking for them to explain their part in the trouble there'd been in the Broken Spoke saloon.

What Millie hadn't told him, because she

hadn't known at the time, was that plans were afoot to replace Lock with Miller, a different man altogether.

In his bedroom at Millie's, Withers had just stripped down his Colt .44 and put it back together. He got up from the bed, which he'd used as a table on which to oil and clean his gun, went to the window and looked out. Most of the evidence of the storm of the day before had disappeared and Main Street was beginning to return to its normal dusty self for the time of year. Had he remained looking out of the window a second longer, he'd have seen Miller step out of his office. But he was disturbed by a knock on his bedroom door. It was Ben Coral, who'd come to tell him the men were ready.

'Right,' Withers said to Coral, who'd been invited to come in. 'I'll meet you all downstairs in the lobby in five minutes.'

When Lock had vacated what had so lately been his office he'd gone straight to the Broken Spoke saloon. The Wanted notice had told him exactly who Cal Withers was and he had guessed what he must have come to

Pecos for. He was going to tell Turner and Norris. There was a big reward on Withers' head and, sheriff or not, he wanted to be the one to claim it. If he was not going to be able to get out of town without making a large donation to the church re-building fund, the reward on Withers' head would go a long way towards compensating him for it.

By the time he stepped into the Broken Spoke the atmosphere in there was beginning to return to normal. Except that Norris was at the bar, still smarting from the beating he'd taken at the hands of Cal Withers and his men. Like everyone else in town Lock had, while collecting together his things in his office, heard the shots coming from the Broken Spoke but he had not known, nor cared particularly, what they were about.

'Zeb,' he greeted Turner, walking up to the bar and standing beside Norris.

Turner barely had the chance to return Lock's greeting, when Norris turned to face Lock.

'You still here?' Norris asked of him contemptuously.

Lock thought he'd seen Norris at his mean-est, but the murderous expression on his face now was worse than anything he'd seen before. It unnerved him to the core.

'I was just leaving,' he muttered to Norris, 'but then I discovered something you guys ought to know.'

Then, looking around to see if Withers was still in the saloon and finding he was not, he added: 'I know who the man you was playing cards with earlier is.'

'I don't care who he is,' Norris snapped back in reply. 'I just want to know what you're still doing here.'

'If you'll listen, I'll tell yer,' Lock replied, full of his own importance. Importance that he hoped would win him favour with Norris.

'I ain't gonna listen to anything,' Norris replied fiercely. 'Just get out of my sight before I kill ya.'

His words were spoken loud enough to carry around the saloon and it again became silent. Norris was aware of the fact and took comfort in knowing people were going to be reminded of just how big a man he was in Pecos. Turner sensed that trouble was brewing and he didn't want it. Not now that Miller was sheriff. He tried to stop it.

'Let him have his say,' he said to Norris, 'and then I'll throw him out.'

Norris didn't say anything in reply but his look told Turner he'd go along with what he suggested.

'All right,' he said, relieved, to Lock. 'Have your say and then get out.'

'He's a wanted bank robber and there's a price of five thousand dollars on his head.'

Both Turner and Norris looked shocked. Turner spoke first.

'How do you know this?' he asked Lock.

'There's a Wanted notice for him in my office. I'd have brought it with me to show you, but Miller came in and I had to leave,' Lock replied, puffed up more than he was before.

'The sonofathievingbitch!' Norris exclaimed. 'Do you mean to tell me I was set upon by a bunch of goddamn, no good longriders?'

'Yeah,' enthused Lock ingratiatingly. 'You was, Norris. How else could they have got away with it?'

Norris thought for a moment. He knew the

eyes of the Broken Spoke's customers were upon him and he was glad that they were listening to Lock's words.

'Right,' he suddenly declared. 'Are they still in town?'

'Sure are,' Lock sang out, in the mistaken belief that his standing was being restored. 'They're staying at Millie's.'

'Let's go and get them, then,' Norris said.

'You're forgetting one thing, Norrie,' Turner informed him, 'Matt here ain't sheriff no more, Miller is.'

At this Lock suddenly looked deflated. Then he said: 'You don't have to be sheriff to claim a reward.'

Norris only needed a fraction of a second to remind himself how much he despised Lock. He turned on him.

'In that case,' he announced, 'we don't need you, do we.'

'That ain't fair, Norrie—' Lock began.

Norris interrupted him.

'You weren't no good to us before, I can't see you'll be any good to us now,' he said, putting his hand on his gun. 'Now you gonna leave or what?'

'That ain't fair, Norrie,' Lock said again, his tone of voice pathetic in the extreme. 'You wouldn't have all this, if it hadn't have been for me.'

'This!' Norris snarled in mocking tones. 'This! What is this?' he asked, throwing his hands up in the air and casting his eyes contemptuously about the saloon.

Lock realized he wasn't going to get anywhere with Norris and decided in his usual cowardly way that it was in his best interests to back off.

'All right,' he said. Then looking at Turner, he added: 'I'll just collect what's mine from the safe.'

'You ain't got nothing in there,' Norris snarled at him between gritted teeth. 'What you had is mine.'

Stunned, Lock looked from Turner to Norris and back to Turner again. The look Turner gave him told Lock he was with Norris.

'But why?' he asked, looking at Turner. 'That's my money. I earned it just like the rest of you earned yours.'

'Yeah,' replied Norris, 'and if you'd been

doing your job as you was paid to, we'd still be earning. But as it is we ain't and what you got in the safe is all forfeit.'

'That ain't fair,' Lock said again, repeating the words for the second time. Like all cowardly opportunists, he couldn't see why things going wrong should be blamed on him.

It incensed Norris even further.

'Ain't fair?' he growled, turning on Lock and pushing his face into his. 'Ain't fair? What's with this "it ain't fair"?'

The people near them began to sense what was coming and stood back. Lock couldn't find an answer.

'Is this fair?' Norris asked, his voice still loud, holding his injured hand up to Lock's face. 'Ben's dead. Is that fair?'

Lock still said nothing. He hadn't known that Kirk had been killed and he realized suddenly that it must have had something to do with the gunshots he'd heard earlier. The news of Kirk's death didn't make him feel grief of any description. It simply made him fear all the more for his own life. But he wanted his money, which he believed he had every right to.

'I gotta get out of town,' he said weakly to Norris, but looking at Turner. 'Town council ordered me to. And I gotta give money to the church rebuilding fund. I need what's in the safe.'

'And I told you it ain't yours no more,' Norris said to him viciously.

Norris was aware of the fact that he had an audience and he played up to it, knowing it would help to restore his reputation.

Lock began to say something in what was still a whining voice, when Norris suddenly pulled out his gun and stuck it under his nose.

'You ain't listening, Matt,' he said to Lock more viciously than ever, 'and I'm getting tired of it. Now, if you're leaving town, I suggest you go now, while you're still able.'

Lock knew he'd lost the argument but he nevertheless looked towards Turner in the vain hope that Turner might come to his aid. But the look on Turner's face told him it wasn't going to happen.

Not saying another word Lock turned and began to walk out of the saloon. If he didn't have any money on him, he thought to himself, the town couldn't expect him to leave any. And there was still the money in the bank in Odessa. He was comforting himself with such thoughts when a shot rang out. It came from Norris's gun and it slammed straight into the back of Lock's head. Norris's temper had finally snapped and his cheating, lying self had taken control.

The customers of the Broken Spoke looked on in horror as Lock fell against the saloon's batwing doors and landed on the plank-walk outside. Norris had committed a cowardly act and in the process had broken one of the unwritten rules of the Wild West. He would gain nothing but contempt for shooting a man in the back, regardless of what people thought of that man.

As he stood holding his smoking gun, Norris was well aware of the wave of disapprobation that was washing over him. He didn't live by anyone's laws; this had been accepted by the lowlife of Pecos, and this was what had allowed him to rob them blind. But even allowing for this he knew his time in Pecos was up. He'd dealt with Lock. Now he turned on Turner. Cocking his gun, he ordered him to walk to the back room, where the safe was.

'Norris,' Turner began, trying to reason with him.

But Norris was not interested.

'Shut up, Zeb,' he snapped, 'before I kill you too.'

They had arrived in the back room.

'What about the man who took your money, Norris? The bank robber. What about him? We could earn ourselves five thousand dollars there?'

'Shut up and open the safe,' Norris ordered Turner, ignoring what had been said.

'Didn't you hear me, Norris?' Turner tried again. 'You can't let him get away with it. Robbing you like that, in front of everyone.'

Norris held his gun up to Turner and cocked the hammer. He didn't say anything but his look spoke volumes.

'This ain't the way, Norris,' Turner tried to say.

'I said shut up,' Norris said again between gritted teeth. 'This is the last time I'm gonna ask. Open the safe.'

Turner fumbled for the key, which he kept

in a hip pocket on the end of a chain attached to a buttonhole of his waistcoat.

'Come on, come on,' Norris ordered him. His impatience sprang from the fact that he feared Miller might appear at any minute.

Turner at last got the key into the safe's lock. He turned it and opened the safe door. While still keeping his gun on him, Norris pushed Turner out of the way and began to remove the bundles of dollar notes that were inside.

'Get me something to put these in,' he said to Turner.

Turner looked around for an old carpetbag he kept lying around. He knew he had better do what Norris ordered while still hoping to reason with him. He found the bag and handed it to Norris. Norris began to fill the bag with the money that was in the safe.

'It ain't all yours, Norrie,' Turner said.

'It is now,' Norris replied, 'unless you're gonna try and stop me. The game's up, Zeb. There ain't nothing left in Pecos for me now and I ain't hanging around to wait for Miller to do whatever it is he intends.'

Turner knew his time in Pecos was also finished.

'Maybe I could come with you, Norrie,' he said. 'There ain't nothing left for me here neither. We could both go together and try and set something up somewheres else.'

Norris turned and looked Turner in the eye. He'd never had cause to despise him the way he had Lock. And they had made a lot of money together. Maybe they could start again someplace else.

'All right,' he said, 'but it ain't gonna be easy getting out of town.'

'I know that,' Turner replied, 'but two stand a better chance than one.'

'All right,' Norris replied, stuffing the last of the money from the safe in the bag. 'We gotta get some horses.'

They decided they'd best leave by the back door. Turner had a shotgun under the counter in the saloon and declared that he was going to get it. Norris told him to hurry.

As he was crossing Main Street to Millie's Hotel, Miller had heard the sound of Norris shooting Lock. Hardly had he taken another pace when he saw Lock come flying through the Broken Spoke's batwing doors and fall on to the plank-walk outside. He could guess what had happened but was unsure of what to do about it. It wasn't that he feared for his own life. It was more that he wanted to do his job of cleaning up the town in an effective way. And that meant having help.

He came to a halt in the middle of Main Street. While he was deciding what to do for the best Cal Withers and his men stepped out of Millie's Hotel. One of the men had gone to the livery stable where the gang had put their horses. The man was standing by the hitching rail outside Millie's with the mounts ready. As they stepped from the plank-walk the gang couldn't help but see Miller standing in the middle of Main Street. Cal Withers recognized him as the man who had been in the hotel two nights before. He could see that he was wearing a sheriff's badge. Certainly he hadn't been wearing one before and he wondered if this was what Millie had meant when she said 'not yet' in reply to his question asking if Miller was somebody important.

After thinking for a moment, Withers simply carried on walking towards his horse. They'd come to rob the bank. If this young sheriff got in their way, they'd kill him. It was that simple. There was no other consideration to be made. His gang followed him and as one they mounted their horses.

Seeing them do so, Miller guessed they must be leaving town. He couldn't see now that he'd get the chance to talk to Withers. Not knowing anything about Withers being a wanted man, he hadn't believed a word of what Norris had told him about the killing of Kirk. Thinking still that Withers might have been of use to him, he was sorry now to see him and his men looking as if they were getting ready to leave town.

Mounted, Cal Withers paused to look at Miller. The bank was situated opposite the Broken Spoke saloon, next to Jim Wood's general store. Still thinking that if Miller got in their way he'd kill him, Cal Withers started his horse off walking.

Miller decided he'd have to go into the Broken Spoke alone to investigate the shooting of Lock. He was thinking that he had no choice but to do the job alone. Kirk was dead. Lock was now also dead. That only left Turner and Norris. Kill Norris, he thought, and Turner would soon put his hands up.

Thinking in this way, he started to walk in the direction of the Broken Spoke. Stepping over Lock's dead body, he went inside just in time to see Turner stand up from bending down to fetch his shotgun. His and Turner's eyes met and a look of panic spread across Turner's face. He didn't know what to do, whether to play the innocent or make a run for it and join Norris. He decided to do the latter. He moved so quickly that he was gone before Miller realized it.

'Quick,' he said to Norris, as he ran back to where Norris was waiting. 'Miller's out front.'

'That sonofabitch!' Norris exclaimed. 'If he tries to stop us, I'll give it to him. Get the door open, Zeb.'

Turner had to fumble again for a key. He did not possess the kind of psychotically crazy nerves that Norris had and was beginning to cave in.

'Come on,' Norris urged him, though secretly hoping that Miller would show his face before they got away. He wanted to kill him.

Turner found the key at last and quickly shoved it into the keyhole. It had never been an easy lock and, being seldom used, was as stiff as ever. At last it turned and he pulled the door open, just in time for Miller to appear coming through the door that led to the saloon. Norris let off a shot. It missed Miller by a whisker, slamming into the door-frame an inch from his face. Miller pulled back. He had his own gun drawn. Gingerly but quickly he peered around the doorway into the room. No one was there. Both Norris and Turner had fled. Miller ran to the back door and carefully poked his head out, just in time to see Norris, preceded by Turner, disappear round the corner at the top of the alley. There was only one place they could go. Main Street. Their path could take them nowhere else.

Miller decided his best bet was to confront them on Main Street. He hurried back through the saloon. In the saloon people were beginning to wonder what exactly was going on. There was no one to serve them at the bar and they'd heard Norris's gun shot. Next Miller appeared, with his gun drawn, and pushing his way through them. One of the more lively of them suggested, if there was no one to serve them, they should help themselves to whatever drink they wanted. No one needed to be told twice and as Miller ran through the batwing doors on to Main Street he was aware of a stampede of feet towards the bar. He was glad of it, believing it might serve to divert the customers away from what was likely to be happening on the street outside. An audience could only make matters worse.

Miller arrived just in time to see Norris appear at the front end of the alley running alongside the Broken Spoke. Norris was quick to let off a shot and Miller had to dive behind a water-butt to take cover. A gun battle ensued with Norris and Miller taking shots at one another but with neither of them hitting their target.

At the same time Cal Withers and four of his men were inside the bank, robbing it. Their sixth man was holding the horses, which were taking fright at the sound of gunfire. He was having a real struggle to hold on to the horses reins.

'What the hell's that?' Cal Withers asked, turning and looking at Bill Coral, who was standing over a teller while he filled a money bag.

Another of Withers' men was pushing the manager of the bank towards a safe, which he, the manager, had been ordered to open.

'Search me,' Coral replied.

'Take a look,' Withers ordered one of his men, Bartlett, who was standing by with his Colt drawn. 'Hurry up and empty that drawer,' he ordered the teller.

Coral pushed his gun deeper into the teller's side to show they meant business.

'Well, what is it?' Withers called to Bartlett.

The man, looking through a window, called back, 'There's a gunfight going on outside. Looks like it's between the sheriff and that card-shark from the saloon.'

'Damn!' Withers cursed out loud.

'Dave can't hold the horses,' Bartlett informed Withers.

'Well, get out there and help him,' Withers ordered him. 'But don't get involved in the gunfight.'

Bartlett did what he was told but was too late to be of any help to Dave. For just as he stepped out of the bank all but one of the horses broke free. They ran off frenziedly down Main Street.

'Goddamnit!' Bartlet cursed, turning and heading back into the bank. 'The horses have gone,' he informed Withers.

Withers and Coral, old hands at robbing banks, looked to one another. They both knew what to do. Finish stuffing the money into bags.

It was obvious to the bank manager things were becoming very confused. He had been emptying the safe into cloth money sacks. He stopped what he was doing.

'Don't,' the gang member who was overseeing him snarled. 'Finish it!'

Thinking the situation could allow him to start being obstructive, the bank manager, refused. Without hesitating, the gang member shot him in the stomach. Withers looked around quickly to see what had happened. It didn't bother him. It was one problem less to deal with.

'Try anything funny and you'll get the same,' Bill Coral snapped at the teller, who'd finished emptying his drawer and who was now standing with his hands held high and shaking all over. 'Get down on the floor.' Coral came round to the front of the bank to stand by Withers. The gang member who'd been overseeing the bank manager empty the safe, grabbed the last of the dollar bundles from it. Then he too hurried to join Withers and Coral on the other side of the bank.

'What we gonna do?' Coral asked Withers.

Withers went to the window and looked out.

'Well no one's shooting at us yet. Maybe we can just walk out of here.'

'But what about the horses?' Bill Coral asked. 'What we gonna ride out of town on?'

Outside the bank on Main Street Norris and Miller still had each other pinned down. Much more of it and Miller knew he'd run out of bullets. But, then, he thought, the same must surely happen to Norris. Turner hadn't fired his shotgun yet but Miller guessed he wouldn't have many cartridges on him.

As Miller was thinking these thoughts, he noticed the horses breakaway from Withers' man's grasp. Then he heard the sound of the gunshot come from inside the bank. Up until then he hadn't realized what was happening in the bank. Now he suddenly knew why Cal Withers and his men had shown up in town. He cursed to himself, realizing he was in a hopeless situation. He needed help. But where was it to come from? And would anyone else in town realize the bank was being robbed?

Still wondering, Miller turned to look at the man who was standing outside the bank holding on to the reins of the one horse that had not got away. He was still struggling. Miller looked down Main Street. The other horses had stopped a hundred yards away and were drinking water from another water-trough.

Miller wasn't the only one who'd realized the bank was being robbed. Norris had, too. He knew it had to be Withers. A smile of grim satisfaction spread across his face. Lock had been right after all and it was going to save his life.

'This is our chance,' he turned and said to Turner. 'Either to get the reward or join forces with that lot over there.'

By 'that lot over there' he meant Cal Withers and his men, for as he spoke they stepped out of the bank on to the plank-walk. Keeping an eye on Miller, Cal Withers looked up and down Main Street. He quickly caught sight of the runaway horses.

'Go get the horses,' he ordered Dave. 'And you go and help him,' he said to one of his other men.

He knew Bartlett was a good shot and wanted to keep him at his side.

Withers looked over at Miller, who'd been taking cover behind the side of the water trough that was facing the bank. Both men still had their guns in their hands and they eyeballed one another. Then, slowly standing up, Miller raised his gun.

'You ain't going nowhere,' he said to Withers.

Withers raised his own gun. So did Bill Coral and the rest of the gang.

'Who says so?' Withers asked.

'Me,' was Miller's reply.

'And whose army?' Withers sneered.

Miller didn't have an answer to Withers' question. As he stood, his eyes darting between Norris and Turner and Withers, he was suddenly gripped by a feeling of despondency. Either Norris and Turner were going to get him or the bank robbers were. He couldn't help but wonder if he should keep his gun trained on Norris and Turner and simply wave Withers and his men on. But somehow he couldn't. It wasn't what he'd pinned the badge on to do.

'Miller,' Norris suddenly called out to him in hushed tones. 'We can help you out of this.'

He counted on Withers and his men not hearing him.

'The only help I want from you,' Miller replied, not bothering to keep his voice down, 'is for you to throw down your guns and come out with your hands up.'

'Don't be stupid,' was Norris's reply. 'Live and you can share the reward. Die and we get it all.'

'Reward?' Miller asked. 'What reward? What are you talking about?'

'Him over there,' Norris replied. 'He's a wanted man. Lock saw his face on a Wanted notice. There's a reward of five thousand dollars on his head. You help us claim it and we'll let you live. Don't and you're dead.'

Miller turned his head to look at Withers. Withers, who hadn't heard what Norris had said, simply looked back at him. Miller despised Norris; there hadn't been time yet for him to hate Withers. If he could only make one of them pay for their crimes against the people of Pecos, he knew which one he'd rather it be. Especially if into the bargain it was going to cost him his own life.

'What's it gonna be, Miller?' Norris, growing impatient for a reply, called out.

'This,' Miller threw back at him. He dropped down behind the water-trough for cover, and fired at him.

'What we gonna do now?' Turner asked Norris.

As he spoke the two men whom Withers had sent to get the gang's horses, had rounded them up and were standing holding them waiting for orders from Withers.

'Stay where you are,' Withers called out to them. 'We'll come to you.'

'They're gonna get away,' Norris, who'd heard what Withers had told his men, called out to Miller. 'Is that what you want?'

Miller didn't make a reply. Instead he cursed to himself. He needed help but where was it ever likely to come from.

'Well?' Norris called out to him.

Still Miller did not reply. He simply turned his head to look at Withers. His and Withers' eyes met. Withers had no cause to feel sorry for the law, in whatever predicament it got itself into. It was lying helpless now in the dust before him. Why should he feel any compunction to offer it, in the form of Miller, a young, inexperienced sheriff, any help at all? None, except that he hated lowlife like Norris, hated his kind more even than he hated the law.

'We're coming out, Miller, to help you,' Norrie suddenly called out, 'so don't shoot.'

'What you talking about, Norrie?' asked Turner, who was standing behind him, pressed up against the wall of the Spoke that was adjacent to the alley. 'Why don't we just make a run for it?'

'Where to?' Norris asked in reply. 'And, besides, we ain't got any horses.'

Turner knew that Norris was right, but still he did not relish the idea of stepping out unprotected on to Main Street. Then Withers spoke.

'All right,' he called out to Norris, knowing that Miller was not going to reply to him. 'You come on out then. Or we're coming in.'

Norris looked at Turner. This wasn't the way things were supposed to be going. He had to think quickly.

'We got money,' he called back to Withers, 'and plenty of it. Why don't we put it all together then we can all get away.'

This gave Withers something to think about. He despised Norris but money was money. It was what they were in Pecos for. To get money. Maybe, he thought, he should just go along with what Norris was suggesting and then a bit further down the line kill him. Whatever, he'd drive a hard bargain.

'Which one of us you trying to do a deal with?' he called out to Norris.

'I'll deal with whoever wants to deal with me. I ain't fussy,' Norris called back.

No, Withers thought to himself cynically, I don't suppose you are.

Miller began to feel even more despondent. His first attempt at enforcing the law and he was failing miserably. He looked at Withers, who was standing tall and fearless on the plank-walk. Withers looked back at him. It felt to Miller as if Withers was looking straight through him, as if he wasn't there. It made him feel small and of no consequence. He thought about his gun. How many bullets were there left in the chamber? He guessed one, maybe two. He decided that whatever happened, whatever the odds, he was not going to go down without using them. If he was going to die, someone was going to die with him. Then he thought of Hannah and his heart swelled with the pain of regret at the thought of what might have been.

'All right, Norris, show us what you've got,' Withers called out.

'I got a bag full of money,' Norris called back.

'Let me see it,' Withers replied.

The bag was at Turner's feet. Norris turned and looked at it.

'What you gonna do?' Turner asked him.

'Well, I ain't just gonna give it to them, am I,' Norris replied. 'But I gotta show it to them.'

He took hold of it.

'All right,' he called out to Withers, holding the bag out in front of him, just enough for it to be seen. 'Here it is.'

'How much is in there?' Withers asked.

'Enough,' was Norris's reply.

Withers looked at Bill Coral. Coral knew the game Withers was playing and the look he returned told Withers to carry on with it.

'Enough? What's enough?' Withers called back.

'Enough, I said,' was Norris's reply. 'How much you got?'

'That ain't the question now, is it,' Withers said. 'You wanna join us? Come on out now.'

Norris looked as if he was ready to do what Withers suggested.

'You ain't just gonna step out there?' Turner asked him.

'You got any better ideas?' Norris replied impatiently.

It was obvious Turner hadn't.

'You can stay here, if you want, Zeb. But I'm not.'

He was just about to step out on to Main Street when Miller suddenly spoke.

'Nobody's going anywhere.'

He spoke with all the courage he possessed and stood tall as any man could. It impressed Withers.

'Well, there's your answer, Norris. Looks like we ain't gotta deal after all,' he called out. 'Come on, men, let's get out of here.'

The two men holding the horses took a step towards Withers.

'Wait,' Norris called out.

'No,' Miller snapped back, 'you wait, Norris. I said there ain't gonna be a deal and that means there ain't gonna be one.'

Miller didn't know where what he was saying was going to lead, he just knew he couldn't sit back and let Norris get away with it. Withers' men continued leading the horses to him and he and Bill Coral stepped off the plank-walk to meet them.

'Do what the sheriff says,' a voice suddenly called out.

It came from an alley running by the side of the bank. Everyone turned to see whose it was. All except Miller, that is. He knew it belonged to Dwight Cash. As they all looked in Cash's direction the barrels of a shotgun, Cash's, was poked out of the alley. They all heard him cock both hammers. The air suddenly filled with an even greater tension than already existed. Miller stepped forward.

'We all gonna die or what?' he asked, his natural courage being reinforced by the help he'd just got.

Without bothering to give a reply, Withers started to fire in Cash's direction, at the same time running to the horses. Bill Coral started to fire, too. Withers mounted his horse before anyone knew what had happened.

'Come on, Bill,' he shouted to Coral, keeping up a stream of fire in Cash's direction.

In an instant Bill Coral had mounted his horse, firing at Cash as he did so. Taking his lead, the rest of the gang mounted their horses.

'Come on,' Withers called to his men, 'let's get out of here.'

Suddenly there was a lull in the gunfire being directed at Cash. Taking advantage of the fact, he broke cover and emptied both barrels of his shotgun in Withers' direction. At the same time Norris fired a shot at Miller. Miller, expecting it, dropped down in front of the water-trough he'd been standing by and the bullet whistled over his head.

The shot that sprayed from Dwight Cash's shotgun had slammed into Withers' left side, knocking him from his horse.

'Cal!' Bill Coral called out, seeing what had happened.

Norris's shot had missed Miller but he now saw what he reckoned was his chance. Shying away in fear, Withers' horse was coming towards him. If he was lucky he'd be able to grab it. Taking the bag of money and firing to keep Miller pinned down, he ran out from the alley. Miller fired at him but he only had two shots left in his gun and they were soon used up. Quickly he began to reload.

As confusion reigned in Main Street, it began to look as if Norris was going to get away after all. He'd given no thought to Turner's escape. Turner watched Norris grab hold of the horse's reins and, managing to keep hold of the bag of money, swing himself up and into the saddle. He didn't care one way or the other about Norris escaping but what he didn't like was seeing his money go with him. Raising his own shotgun he took aim and began to squeeze the trigger.

Mounted squarely on Withers' horse, Norris took one last look at Miller and he hated him for being, as he saw it, the cause of all his troubles. He could see him shoving bullets into the chamber of his gun. He was holding the bag of money with his good hand and the reins and his gun with his bad. Withers' horse didn't like the stranger who had suddenly mounted him and the animal wasn't going to make it an easy ride for him. As it began to stamp its feet and buck, Norris tried successfully to fix the moneybag by its handles to the horn of the saddle. Next he swapped his gun from his bad hand to his good and pointed it at Miller and fired. Had Withers' horse not bucked wildly at the moment the gun's hammer thumped into the bullet he'd have hit Miller but as it was the shot went wide and, hissing, flew into the water trough Miller was leaning against. This gave Miller the chance he needed. He'd finished reloading his gun. He snapped the barrel and chamber back into place, raised it and fired in Norris's direction. He hit him in the chest. At the moment he did so, the pellets from Turner's shotgun peppered Norris's side. He fell heavily to the ground, dying. Glad to be rid of its unwanted burden, Withers' horse ran off down Main Street at a gallop.

Withers himself was still lying in the dirt of Main Street. He'd quickly collected himself and, having managed to hold on to his gun, was firing in Cash's direction. Bill Coral quickly came to his aid, calling him to get up. Cash had to reload. While he was doing so Withers managed to get to his feet. Coral was there for him and he tried to mount Coral's horse behind the saddle. The rest of the gang kept up a barrage of fire that splintered the wood of the bank's wall behind which Cash was taking cover.

The air was full of turmoil and bullet shot. Withers, who was bleeding badly and beginning to weaken helplessly, found it a struggle to remain seated behind Bill Coral. Coral's horse, nearly demented by the noise and confusion around it, wanted to shake this new and extra burden off but Coral wasn't going to let it.

'Hold on, Cal,' he shouted to Withers. 'Hold on!'

Fighting to keep his horse under control, Coral half-turned round to take hold of Withers by the shirt to stop him from sliding off. But it was no use. Withers, beginning to slip into unconsciousness, was too heavy for him. Coral knew it was useless and loosening his grip, he let Withers go. Miller, turning from having just shot Norris, saw it happen. He raised his gun again, aimed it at Coral and fired twice. Both shots hit home and Coral, dead in an instant, fell from his horse, landing a few feet from Withers. The rest of the gang, seeing they were now leaderless, fled.

Suddenly remembering Turner, Miller turned on his heels to face the alley in which Turner had taken cover. Something told him Turner wasn't there. Looking up, he saw him running away down Main Street.

'Let him go,' he heard Cash's voice call out. 'Let him go.'

Miller turned to see Dwight Cash step on to Main Street. He looked from him back to Turner, just in time to see Turner disappear up an alley between Millie's Hotel and the building next to it.

'You all right?' he heard Cash ask.

'Guess so,' he said turning to look at him and then to the spot where Bill Coral and Cal Withers, now dead, were lying. 'Thanks to you,' he added.

Both men looked at one another.

'I wanted the town cleaned up just as much as you did, Mitch. And now it is,' was all Cash said in reply.

Before Miller could say anything more, the sound of hoofs pounding the dirt was suddenly heard. Both men looked down Main

Street in time to see Turner heading at a gallop out of town.

'Guess that just about seals it,' Cash remarked.

Miller simply looked at him and smiled.

In the next few moments Main Street began to fill with people. Amongst them was Jim Wood and Tom Cowell.

'We sure picked the right man,' Cowell said as he approached Miller.

'I told you,' Jim Wood said in reply.

Before anyone else could say anything Hannah Voegel came bursting out of the crowd, which was beginning to throng around Miller and Dwight. As Miller embraced her, the citizens of Pecos looked on with admiration and gratitude.

Word soon spread that Miller had not just rid the town of Norris, but that he'd foiled a bank robbery into the bargain. Dwight Cash was allowed to claim the price that was on Withers' head but it was donated to the Reverend Tapper's church fund. With that and the money retrieved from Norris's and Turner's carpetbag Pecos built itself a church that to this day remains the pride of Texas.